## "You just used me to make her jealous!"

Janna's furious words didn't disturb Peter. He leaned back in his seat. "That was a bonus," he said cheerfully.

Perhaps, but Peter had used the situation to anger Caroline into breaking her engagement to him. That wasn't kind, but then he wasn't a kind man. "Why didn't you just tell her you were tired of her?" Janna demanded.

"I wasn't, until she started discussing honeymoons," he explained.

Janna couldn't contain her next remarks. "You probably did her a favor. She must be glad she's rid of a man like you! You strike me as being a rotten matrimonial risk!"

Peter smiled slightly. "For Caroline—yes." He looked deeply into Janna's eyes. "For another woman—who knows?"

# OTHER
# *Harlequin Romances*
## by JANE DONNELLY

# Behind a Closed Door

by

## JANE DONNELLY

*Harlequin Books*

TORONTO • LONDON • NEW YORK • AMSTERDAM
SYDNEY • HAMBURG • PARIS

Original hardcover edition published in 1979
by Mills & Boon Limited

ISBN 0-373-02270-0

Harlequin edition published July 1979

# CHAPTER ONE

'Do me a favour?' asked Betsy Byers, a plump and pretty girl in her early twenties, with reddish hair and a country-fresh complexion, putting down the phone she had just answered.

'Of course,' said the other girl, who was emerging from a small changing cubicle with a dress a customer had decided not to buy. 'What?' She replaced the dress on the rail and Betsy laughed.

'You should say "What?" first. Remember the donkey.'

There was an old donkey in Joanna's paddock, because a couple who had moved from the village into Birmingham had asked if they could leave him there until they decided what to do with him. There wasn't much they could do as they were going into a flat, and everybody knew that Joanna was burdened with Freddy for his remaining years. There was also a tatty budgerigar that had landed on her windowsill one morning, and her dog and cat had both started off life as rejects.

If anything, or anybody, was in trouble Joanna Wyman would rush to rally round, but she had no complaints that her friends took advantage. She had good friends, and Betsy was one of the best.

Life was good, Joanna felt. Even business was good.

Her business was a second-hand clothes shop. One of those bright little establishments that are opening and flourishing these days, where everything is so nearly new that the naked eye can't spot the difference. Her county set customers brought in couture models they had bought on impulse and regretted later, or evening dresses or eye-catching outfits that they had only worn a few times. Other women brought in clothes that had proved to be the wrong size, or shape, or colour; but might be just what somebody else was looking for, especially at half the price.

Her shop was attached to her black-and-white cottage, and had once been the village blacksmith's forge. For most of Joanna's life it was her father's studio. He had painted, Cotswold scenes mostly, and taught art at a comprehensive school. Until eight months ago when he had died, suddenly, with no warning at all; and although she had friends she had no other family.

Until then she had worked in a dress shop in Broadway, coming back to the village each night and preparing the evening meal for herself and her father. But the first night she came back from work to an empty house all her courage had crumbled and she had cried herself sick.

Betsy had been watching out for her, and had followed her into the house within a few minutes, going into the kitchen to put on the kettle, and offering a wad of tissues and a shoulder to cry on.

'Andy and I think you ought to make a change,' Betsy had said, when Joanna was nearer herself again, and the tea had been poured out. 'We think you need something you can pitch into—a real challenge.'

'What sort of challenge?'

'You've got a head for business.' At twenty-one Joanna was managing the shop where she worked. 'Why don't you set up on your own?'

That was how it started. The forge was a natural for some sort of shop and they wondered about a restaurant, because Joanna was a good cook. But meals for holiday-makers would have been seasonal, while clothes were in demand all year round, and so, a couple of months later, 'Janna's Place'—which had always been her pet name—opened as a nearly-new shop.

Stocks were small to start, but the word spread, and within months the racks were carrying a good selection of suits and coats, dresses and separates. There were shoes and handbags on the shelves, and pieces of costume jewellery in glass-fronted wall cabinets.

It was a delightful little shop, and just the place for picking up bargains. Janna made friends of her customers —less from a profit motive than because she liked most of the people she met—and she now had a regular clientele.

She was an attractive girl, with fine bones and a pretty intelligent face. Her dark hair, parted down the middle, was silky and healthy. Her eyes were green, flecked with brown, ranging from warm hazel to glinting green according to her moods. They were usually hazel, and her wide mouth was usually ready to smile.

She smiled now. 'So what is it you want me to do?'

'Help me to cook dinner tomorrow night,' said Betsy. Betsy's domestic talents were patchy. She was a first-class needlewoman, and had been doing alterations for Janna's Place ever since it opened. She was brisk and thorough with the housework. The apartment she and her husband Andrew shared in what had once been the vicarage was spotless, and she also housekept the top floor. But she didn't like cooking, and she called on Janna whenever anything special was needed.

Janna's cooking had flair. She cut out recipes from magazines and read cookbooks for pleasure, and since there was only herself to cook for at home these days she was glad her boy-friend lived alone and only five minutes away. She cooked for him most days, and of course she would help Betsy tomorrow night.

The phone call had been from Andrew, Betsy's husband, articled to a firm of solicitors, so it was probably a business date. 'You don't have anything planned, do you?' Betsy asked anxiously, and Janna made a small grimace.

'As usual,' she said, 'no.' Her boy-friend wasn't one for gadding about. He had dedication, and in many ways he reminded her of her father, which was why she had fallen for him in the first place.

'It's Peter,' said Betsy, and when Janna looked blank, 'Peter *Craig*.'

'Oh, him,' said Janna.

'Why be like that,' and Janna was being unreasonable, 'when you don't even know him.'

'I don't really want to know him,' said Janna.

'He's all right,' said Betsy, repeating something she had often said. 'He's been very decent to us.' It was Peter Craig's firm to which Andrew was articled, and it was his house in which they lived. He had bought the rambling old vicarage and had it turned into four flats, keeping the top one for himself. Andrew and Betsy lived on the first floor and Betsy was Peter Craig's housekeeper.

It was an easy job, he was based in London. When he used the flat she provided the occasional meal for him and kept the freezer stocked, but mostly he ate out. His girl-friend seemed to use the apartment more than he did.

Janna was no prude. It was none of her business, and it wasn't the women in the flat she found distasteful. It was because she disliked the kind of man he was. She had never met him, but she knew enough about him to be sure of that.

He was a very tough ambitious lawyer, earning in the top one per cent bracket of his profession, and Andrew could still hardly believe his luck in getting into such a successful firm. Peter Craig's name was a byword for knowing every twist and turn of the law and every trick of the trade, so that most of the cases his staff handled they won.

Andrew would never be Craig's equal, because Andrew lacked ruthlessness. He became personally involved in some of the clients' troubles, his sympathies were often stirred, while Craig was always cold and calculating.

Janna thought that Andrew's boss sounded more like a machine than a man and she had no wish to meet him, no matter how charming and witty and generous he might be in private life. Betsy said he was all that, but Janna didn't care for heartless people with more than their share of surface charm. She was a good judge of character, a believer in empathy, and she knew that she and Peter Craig would have no points of contact.

So, although he had been coming and going in the Old Vicarage for the last six months, and Betsy and Andrew saw him constantly and they were Janna's very good friends, she wouldn't have recognised him if she had fallen over him. And that wasn't likely to happen. Peter Craig kept on his feet, a jump ahead of the rest of the field.

'What sort of meal?' she asked, and Betsy said,

'Well, he's here tomorrow night, and it seems it's his birthday and Andy's just asked him if he'll have dinner with us, and he's said he will.'

'That's big of him,' muttered Janna. 'I should have thought he'd be celebrating his birthday with two blondes and a magnum of champagne.'

'Well, he isn't,' said Betsy. 'Why don't you and Allan come along?'

'To the birthday party?'

'It isn't a birthday party. But we're all neighbours and you might like him if you met him.'

Janna looked stubborn. She would not like him. But she said, 'Thanks anyway, I'll ask Allan. What sort of meal?'

'Oh, something a bit special, you know the sort of thing,' said Betsy, who enjoyed eating although she wasn't fond of cooking.

A Daimler drew up outside and two women got out,

one carrying a suitcase. 'Lovely,' said Janna, 'it's Mrs Morrison-Jones, I do hope the rich will always be with us.'

Mrs Morrison-Jones' husband owned a large hotel, and she had a large dress allowance. But she was an impulsive buyer and when she got her purchases home she often realised she had made a mistake. Also she believed she was a size twelve although she was a fourteen. She breathed in, and held herself tight and straight in front of changing room mirrors, and then couldn't understand why it didn't seem quite 'her' in front of her own mirrors in her own bedroom. She was always bringing beautiful clothes that Janna was delighted to buy because she had other customers who would love them. Today there was a black velvet trench coat, soft and supple, that fitted Mrs Morrison-Jones too snugly; and a cream silk dress she had tired of.

She unloaded both, and bought a grey French pleated skirt that needed a slight adjustment on the waistband. Betsy promised it for tomorrow and took it away, pinned up, to do the alteration.

The next free moment she had Janna got out her cookbooks and sat with them on a big old wooden chest, making notes of suggestions and a list of page numbers, so that she could discuss tomorrow night's menu with Betsy later.

Customers came, chatted, tried on, brought things and bought things. When they saw what she was doing the good cooks told her their own favourite recipes, and she jotted down some of them—sometimes because they sounded interesting, sometimes from politeness. For instance, she didn't think that a fish stew was what Betsy had in mind, but the lady who liked it was a regular customer, so Janna said, 'Sounds fascinating,' and scribbled away.

With a pâté for starters—she could make that tonight —and something in the fruit line to finish the meal, and cheese of course, she could concentrate on the main course. Something with a super sauce or an out-of-the-ordinary casserole. If she could persuade Allan to come along she would accept the invitation and finally meet Peter Craig. If she was cooking the meal she might as well help to eat it.

She closed at her usual time, five o'clock, and went through the connecting door into the living room of her cottage. It was a comfortable room, low beams, inglenook fireplace, easy chairs covered in cabbage rose chintz and rugs on a polished wood floor.

All the furniture had been here since her mother and father bought it at auction sales when they were newlyweds. It fitted, it suited, her father had never wanted to change it and neither did Janna. Because although her mother had died when she was just into her teens she had had a happy childhood, and the rooms in this house had always sheltered her with love.

It had been a wrench changing the studio, but it would have been heartrending to keep it as it was when her father had painted there and, just as Betsy and Andrew had said, opening her own shop had been the challenge she needed to carry her over the first weeks after his death. And it promised to be a success; she had never regretted her decision.

Punch, a dog who was mostly whippet, met her, wagging his tail. She lived alone, but there was always a welcome from the animals. Judy the cat would be in the little patch of garden, or up one of the trees, and even the donkey—the newcomer, he had only moved into the paddock four weeks ago—broke into a trot to reach the gate when Janna and Punch came out into the garden.

They all wanted feeding and petting, but there was affection too. In the case of the dog there was adoration. He thought the whole world revolved around his mistress.

She ate her meal in the kitchen, salad and a slice of pie. It was a warm evening, very still and quiet, and she turned on the radio and talked to Punch; and kept an eye on the clock because at six-thirty she would be taking a basket of food to Allan's cottage, just across the green.

Allan and her father had so much in common. They had worked on the staff of the same school—her father as head of the arts department and Allan Haines teaching English—although Janna hadn't met Allan before her father died. He had been in lodgings then, several miles away from the village, and her father had never brought him home.

All the staff were kind when her father died, everyone was kind, but Allan came to see her several times during those first numb days after the funeral. He was a slim young man, slight and grave, with beautiful grey eyes and long lashes that were wasted on a man, and they talked about her father.

Allan had admired him tremendously, both as a man and as an artist, and Allan understood about artists because, although he earned his living teaching, marking exercises and papers, he was a writer. He was working on a book now, and that was another reason why Janna felt an affinity with him.

She needed someone to encourage. All her life she had said, 'I like that,' looking at her father's paintings. Every new picture had been exciting, a small adventure. Now there weren't paintings any more, but there was Allan's book, and when they weren't talking about her father they'd talked about that. It all helped to fill the emptiness of bereavement.

It was strange how things had worked out. Janna had always had boy-friends, but none that she would have considered leaving home for. She wouldn't have left her father for any man she had met and now, when he wasn't here any more, Allan had come along, and she told herself that her life hadn't changed so very much after all.

She spent a little while now, checking the day's accounts. Then she took off the with-it dress and the pretty Italian shoes and got into a pair of jeans and a pink T-shirt. It was relaxing to change into jeans and sneakers after work.

If Allan should feel like going out she could soon nip back and re-glamorise herself, but it was much more likely that he would want to stay put. He might not even want her staying with him, and she would understand that. She would smile, as she used to smile when her father said, 'Close the door as you go out, poppet.'

Allan worked until all hours, just as her father once had. Even when night fell her father would paint on by artificial light because he always said that he carried the colours in his head, and Allan was the same about his writing. His mind was full of the characters and the scenes in his book, and he knew that he was writing a best-seller.

If Allan was immersed in work she and Punch would take a longer walk, along the lanes, because it really was a beautiful evening. The almond trees were in bright pink blossom in front of the church, and the gardens of the houses were full of red and yellow gillyflowers, purple pansies, lilac and lily of the valley.

The new vicarage was a neat modern house built in the grounds of the old, which stood further back from the road, rising four storeys high. That dated from early Victorian days when congregations were larger, and church and vicarage were the social as well as the spiritual centres of the village. But it had been a white elephant for years, and finally the new vicarage was built and the old one was put on the market. Everybody expected it to be demolished to make room for smaller houses, but Andrew mentioned it in the office and Peter Craig had come out to see, liked what he had seen, and bought the place.

From outside it was almost unchanged. There had been pointing and painting. The gardens were now velvet lawns, and there were garages round the back. Windows had been fitted with double glazing, but they still looked like the old windows.

Outside it looked the way it always had, but inside were apartments designed for modern living. Andrew and Betsy loved theirs. They had had a tiny cottage before Peter Craig offered them first choice—well, not quite first, he wanted the top floor himself—at a very reasonable rent.

The rooms were spacious and light, the kitchen a dream, bathroom and fittings all very luxurious, and after her one-up-one-down, with the tiny kitchenette and bathroom tacked on in what used to be a coalshed and a wash-house, Betsy had been over the moon.

She still was and probably always would be. With two bedrooms and a little boxroom they could rear a family here, and grow older and retire, without finding anywhere that suited them better. When Andrew had asked if Betsy could think of somebody suitable to look after Peter Craig's apartment she had said, 'I will. It's the least I can do.'

Until then Betsy had worked in a chemist's shop in town, doing dressmaking in her spare time, but with the salary Peter Craig was offering—and later what Janna paid her for alterations—she no longer needed to go into town to earn a living.

With Craig away so much it turned out to be a caretaking job more than a housekeeping one. Betsy enjoyed keeping his apartment in order, because everything in it was special. All Peter Craig's furniture was the best of its kind. 'Come and see,' she had urged Janna, again and again, but Janna never had.

It would have sounded daft if she had said to Betsy, 'I liked it up there the way it was,' because nobody in their right mind could mean that. But the vicarage had been a rambling, inconvenient old mock-Gothic house, with two turret windows on the top floor. If you stood in those little round towers you could see all over the village, into the gardens and over the fields.

When Janna was a child her mother and the wife of a vicar, who had moved from here years and years ago, were friends. They had had tea together on afternoons when Janna was allowed to play in the old nurseries on the top floor, with old forgotten toys: a dusty dolls' house peopled by peg dolls, a rocking horse without a tail.

She had pretended she was a princess, waiting at her turret window, for a prince to come riding by on a high white charger, so that she could gallop away with him, on the rocking horse without a tail.

The attics were cleared one day, by a dealer in bygone toys, and the money went towards the church's zooming electricity bills. The present vicar and his family had only used the two bottom floors, and were delighted to move into their new house. But like everybody else Janna had been relieved that the old place wasn't pulled down. It was a landmark if nothing else, and it was good that it was now four beautiful homes.

But she still looked up at the turrets sometimes and remembered the magic of the nurseries. She didn't want to see them changed into a gracious-living background for Peter Craig. She preferred to remember them as they were.

When they were offered their apartment Andrew and Betsy had had a cottage for sale, and as soon as Janna had told him the price they were asking Allan had snapped it up. She had known him about eight weeks then, and she was glad he was coming to live in the village.

She hadn't the heart for going out those days. She was

saying no to the young men who had dated her, pleading work, and Allan was a serious young man who didn't want a social life. He said the cottage was exactly what he had been looking for. He had been living in town, but the country was obviously better for a serious writer. That was what he wanted to be and would be too. He was unpublished as yet, but the book was going well.

Allan moved into the cottage as Betsy and Andrew moved out, the same day, and the four of them had a housewarming in the apartment with a celebration bottle of wine, waiting to hear the bell that meant the fish and chip van—that came round the village every Friday night—had reached the green. When they heard it Allan dashed out and bought four portions.

It was more like a picnic than a dinner party. Half the packing cases were still half full. There wasn't nearly enough furniture to fill the big rooms, but Betsy was bouncing with glee, giggling at everything.

This was the first time they had made a foursome. Except for what Janna had told her all Betsy and Andrew knew about Allan Haines was that he had worked with Janna's father, and that he had sufficient capital to buy their cottage. He seemed a nice enough fellow, they thought, very good-looking, Betsy decided, but he didn't have much personality. He was taking most of Janna's spare time and he didn't seem to be exactly cheering her up.

She had lost weight since her father died, she would be prettier when she had regained the few pounds, and it hollowed her cheekbones quite dramatically. Her smooth dark hair made her face look paler without the blusher she wore while she was working, and Betsy decided that she smiled less when she was with Allan.

The evening wasn't such a success that anyone made much effort to repeat it. Janna noticed too that Allan didn't take to Andrew and Betsy. He was polite, he talked, he even said the fish and chips were good, but he couldn't understand how thrilled Betsy was with her new home, dancing around the rooms with half a mugful of Sauternes, saying, 'Isn't it beautiful, though? Isn't it just absolutely out of this world?'

As he walked with Janna back to her home he commented, 'Betsy seems a rather childish young woman. I'm surprised you're such good friends.'

'Betsy is as bright as they come,' Janna had said. 'I'm very fond of her.'

Five months had passed since then and although Janna was often across at Betsy's place, and saw Allan almost every day, there hadn't been another get-together with Andrew and Betsy.

'Let's go out and have a meal together,' Betsy would say, or Janna would suggest, 'Why don't we go down to the coast for the day?' But that was as far as it got. No firm arrangements were ever made.

Allan was comfortably settled in his cottage now. Most nights when he'd finished his school paper work he got down to his writing—just as Janna's father had to his painting. From the beginning they had slipped into the routine of Janna bringing Allan what were described as her 'leftovers', or asking him over to supper.

It was a quiet relationship. He told her that he had fallen in love with her the first time he saw her. Her heartbreak had almost broken his heart. 'You're so beautiful,' he would say, and perhaps she had fallen in love too, because he was the only man in her life.

Tonight Punch trotted across the green ahead of her to the centre door of a row of three cottages. He knew this was where they were coming, although he would have trotted on happily if Janna hadn't stopped.

She had acquired Punch—the runt of an unwanted litter—a couple of years ago, and he had never taken to Allan. He always showed his teeth if Allan pushed him off the settee and sat down beside Janna himself and as Allan admitted he never had cared much for dogs it was reciprocal dislike. When Allan was round at Janna's Punch kept a bright eye on him, and unless there was pouring rain when they came over here Punch preferred to lie outside the door and wait for Janna to come out again. He was never really comfortable in Allan's house.

Janna was—very comfortable. She tapped on the door and Allan answered, 'Come in.' He was going through a reference book he had taken out of the library yesterday, and making notes, but he put the book aside and got up to kiss her. 'Is it that late?'

She forgave him for not noticing how time was passing, her father never did, and she put out the salad and pie she had brought him. As he ate it she said, 'Betsy and Andy want us to have dinner with them tomorrow night.'

'Not me,' said Allan.

'I'm cooking it.'

'That makes a difference.' When he smiled she always wanted to reach out and hold his hand. 'But just at the moment,' he said, 'I couldn't stand Betsy's nattering.'

Betsy was a chatterbox, although Janna could match her and often did. Not with Allan, though. Perhaps because he had said, 'I love your silences. I can be with you and there's no intrusion.'

She had been quiet, subdued, when he said that, full of grief. As passing time began to heal she stayed the way he loved her, when she was with him.

According to Betsy Allan had no sense of humour, and it was true that he didn't find life funny. Nor was it really, not these days, although Janna often laughed when she wasn't with him.

Artists of course were different, special, more sensitive than ordinary folk. Allan was immersed in his book right now, and Janna was quite relieved because she didn't fancy this particular dinner party.

She said, 'They've asked Peter Craig for a meal. It's his birthday.'

'Oh, him.' Allan sounded just as Janna had. He wasn't impressed by what he'd heard of Craig either. Someone as cold-blooded as Craig was not his kind of person. 'You go if you want to, of course,' he said.

'I don't think so,' said Janna. 'I promised to do the cooking, but I'll probably leave Betsy with the last-minute instructions.'

She began to tidy up, unobtrusively, a girl who liked to help, then she said, 'I'd better be away, I've got a pâté to prepare,' and Allan asked,

'Why can't Betsy learn to cook herself?'

'You know she can cook.' Janna was picking up some crumpled sheets of paper that had missed the litter bin, and dropping them into it. She smiled, 'Andy hardly looks undernourished.' Andy, like Betsy, was on the plump side. 'But she's not so fond of the fripperies as I am. I enjoy putting on a spread.'

Allan looked doubtful. 'Well, don't let her put on you,' and Janna chortled,

'Who? *Betsy?*' Betsy gave so much, in time, in support, in friendship, and this was only a little favour she was asking. But it was comforting that Allan was concerned for Janna, and Janna never stopped to realise how ironic this particular concern was when she was cooking for him almost every day.

Punch was waiting, with wagging tail, just outside the door, and Allan walked across the green with them, and stood waiting while they went up the little lane towards the black and white cottage, with its swinging sign 'Janna's Place'.

Punch was happy, leaving Allan behind, and Allan never could see what Janna saw in the animal, ugly jealous little devil.

Janna made the pâté mould that evening. Tomorrow,

when it was turned out, it would look quite professional with its layers of consommé, pâté, cream cheese and chives. She made a list of the items she would need for the meal. She would have to dash into town to buy them, the village store was not for specialist shopping. It should be a delicious meal, and next morning when Betsy said, 'You will be staying, won't you?' she said regretfully,

'Well no, Allan's on a sticky patch in his book and he hates having his concentration broken.'

'Then you come,' said Betsy, and Janna hesitated again. But she decided against it.

'Your guest might not care to have a strange woman plonked down beside him when he's only expecting Andy and you, and—no, I don't think so, thanks very much, though. I'll leave everything ready and perhaps another time.'

The men should have arrived around seven o'clock. Just after half six Betsy and Janna were in the kitchen. Janna had changed into jeans and shirt and was wearing a large striped apron, while Betsy was pretty as a picture in a cotton tiered dress, in lilac and rose pink, with a ribbon tie at the throat.

The pâté mould was turned out on a bed of crisp lettuce, and Janna was stirring the red wine, redcurrant jelly and sour cream, for the sauce to go with the lamb, when Andrew called Betsy's name. 'We're here,' called Andrew.

'They're early,' said Betsy indignantly. 'Oh well, you'll have to meet Peter now.'

'*No!*' hissed Janna. She looked dishevelled, hardly any make-up, and pink and sticky from hanging over a hot stove, and she was determined not to be introduced to Peter Craig in this state.

Normally she wouldn't have minded being caught at a slight disadvantage, appearances weren't all that important, but she wasn't having him looking down his nose at her. In any case she didn't want to meet him.

'Tell me when the coast's clear,' she said, 'and I'll get out.'

Any moment Andrew would have opened the kitchen door, but Betsy forestalled him. She slipped through, her voice gay and welcoming. 'Hello, happy birthday, how lovely to see you!'

Janna heard the man's voice, as Betsy closed the door. It was as warm as Betsy's, and as smiling. 'Bless you for asking me.'

Then the door shut, and Janna went on stirring her sauce.

As they were half an hour early Peter Craig might just have looked in on the way up to his own apartment. When he went she could get away. Or he'd want to go and wash his hands, or into the little boxroom Andy used as an office, to talk work for a few minutes. The kitchen opened into the living-dining area, and there was no other way out of the apartment. Unless she risked leaping like Tarzan for a horse-chestnut tree.

Betsy came in to carry out the pâté and said, 'This is stupid. We're just sitting down. Come on out and say hello.'

'Doesn't he even want to go to the bathroom?'

'Doesn't seem to,' said Betsy, 'and I don't fancy suggesting it.'

'I look such a sight!'

Betsy began to laugh. 'Shall I smuggle you a dress in?' She picked up the pâté plate and said, 'I'd like to introduce my friend Janna. She's in fashion. Some of the very best designers.'

'I shall stay in here and eat,' Janna decided. 'You can leave me some of that for a start. How long are you expecting him to stay?'

'Not long,' Betsy assured her. 'He's driving to Manchester tonight. So he won't be drinking much, or you could have come out after a few glasses and hoped he'd see you in a rosy glow.'

'You can leave me a glass of wine too,' said Janna.

Betsy's kitchen was in mellow Scandinavian pine, a very pleasant room. They ate in here, unless they had company like Peter Craig, and the window overlooked lawned gardens and the rising Cotswold hills. Janna didn't mind at all spending the evening in the kitchen; she often had, although never alone before.

But this was ridiculous. What she should have done was walk out at once and say, 'How do you do, and I'm on my way.' Now she was stuck, and she had to make the best of it. Even Andrew didn't know she was in here, he'd think it was a scream when they told him—Janna trapped in the kitchen and scared to come out.

She kept to the side of the room that was shielded when the door opened; and Betsy loaded the trolley from the dining table, uncharacteristically insisting that she needed no help from Andrew in pushing it, or reloading it in the kitchen.

As Janna was preparing ahead everything went like clockwork. Peter Craig might have imagined this was how the Byers household always operated, but Andrew was very surprised.

Janna had the main course served, and the switchover of plates was made while Betsy tried again. 'Do come in. What does it matter if you're not dressed up to the nines? You look fine, honestly.'

'I'll stick it out now,' said Janna. 'I'm more use in here. I'll do the washing up for you.' From Betsy's expression she suspected that Betsy was about to tell the two men, and she said fiercely, '*No*, and I mean that. I'll be furious if you say a word.'

'Don't bang down anything, then,' Betsy advised, and went back biting her lip to stop herself laughing.

Perhaps Betsy could have prevented Andrew following her in when she came for the coffee, but he did follow, and almost dropped the dishes he was carrying. '*Janna!*' he bellowed. 'What the hell are you doing in here?'

Peter Craig would certainly have heard that. 'Making coffee,' said Janna.

'So I see,' said Andrew, 'but what are you hiding from?'

'You might well ask,' said Betsy, and Janna wasn't confessing that she was keeping out of Peter Craig's way. She shot Betsy a warning glance and said,

'It's like this—I'm starting a sideline. Cooking in the evenings, this sort of thing, small dinner parties, buffets. I'm doing a practice run tonight.'

'Good lord!' said Andrew. 'Betsy said you were giving her a hand, but I didn't realise you were still here.'

'Working behind the scenes,' said Janna demurely. 'Unobtrusive efficiency.'

'Oh yes?' said Andrew, grinning.

'And free to you, of course,' said Janna. 'As this is in the nature of a try-out. If it's a success then I shall start advertising.'

'It's a success,' said Andrew, who couldn't decide whether they were pulling his leg. 'Come and meet my boss.'

Peter Craig got up as Janna came slowly out of the kitchen and said, 'It was a superb meal.'

'So they knew I hadn't cooked it,' said Betsy chirpily.

He was tall, broad-shouldered, loose-limbed. He had an almost boyish face although he was thirty-four today, nice-looking, open. He didn't look over-tough either, just average.

'This is Peter Craig,' said Betsy. 'Peter, Joanna Wyman.'

They shook hands and his grip was firm, cool fingers closing over hers and releasing them immediately. 'Janna's Place?' he said.

'Yes.' Andrew had called her Janna. Perhaps Peter

Craig knew that she and Betsy were friends.

Andrew pulled another chair to the table and Janna was sitting next to Peter, while Betsy went back into the kitchen for another cup and started to pour the coffee.

'You missed a good dinner,' said Andrew, grinning broadly. 'You should have shown yourself.'

'I finished off the pâté and toast,' said Janna. 'It was very nice, I thought.'

'Are you serious, about cooking professionally?' Peter was asking her, and she had to say she was, adding,

'But it's just an idea at the moment. I was trying it out tonight, seeing if I could cope.'

'And why not?' Betsy's lips were twitching. 'She has a talent for it, hasn't she? It has to be something you're born with, because we both took Domestic Science at school, making the same things from the same menus, measuring them just the same, and putting them into the same oven. And I never did get a sponge cake to rise, but Janna's were always light as a feather.'

'You're too kind,' said Janna. They were piling this on too thick, but even a lawyer couldn't prove she wasn't here semi-professionally.

Betsy gulped down a giggle. 'And shall you be charging Allan?'

'Free for friends,' said Janna lightly.

'Who's Allan?' asked Peter.

'Allan Haines, who bought our cottage,' Andrew explained. 'He's a teacher.'

Peter didn't seem to know anything about Allan. He had never shown any interest in the village. This house was an investment and a lodging for him, he didn't get involved with the people living around, and Janna said,

'And a writer,' because she was proud of Allan, and when the book came out perhaps Peter Craig would remember the name.

'What has he written?' he enquired.

'He's writing a book,' she said. 'That's why he bought the cottage.'

'He gets his inspiration round here?' He looked as though he meant Janna and she said shortly,

'He gets peace and quiet around here.'

'And free cooking?' He was smiling, and she shrugged because perhaps he wasn't being insolent. His smile was disarming. 'He's a lucky man,' he said, and she found herself responding to his charm. He didn't look in the least as she had expected him to. She had had a mental picture of a man with cold grey eyes, and a keen hawk-like face.

Peter Craig looked friendly. There were laughter lines at the corner of his eyes, and he was very good company. They talked and laughed. He had a host of anecdotes, a fund of amusing conversation and Janna could under-stand why he was never short of a girl-friend.

'You like it here?' she asked. Dusk had fallen and Betsy had lit the candles on the table. The scent of a posy of lilies of the valley seemed to fill the room, and outside the only sound was the occasional bellow of Farmer West's bull at the other end of the village, and once or twice the braying of Janna's donkey Freddy.

Peter Craig said he liked it very much. It was a pity the house had to be altered so radically inside, but changing times dictated that. Nobody wanted or could afford to live in it the way it was.

Betsy looked around her beautiful room and said that surely it was better to have four homes in the Old Vicarage than one. Anyhow, for years, the two top floors hadn't been used at all.

'They were nurseries right at the top,' said Janna. 'When I was very small I used to play in them some-times.' She smiled at the gentle memories, her mother downstairs, the dolls' house, the rocking horse. 'There were old toys in there that would have fetched a fortune if they'd held on to them for another ten years,' she added. 'As it was they brought in quite a sum.'

Betsy nodded. She remembered the clearing out of the Vicarage nurseries. 'There was a dolls' house,' Janna reminisced, 'I'd have dearly loved. I suppose everything was gone?' She turned to Peter.

'Sadly yes,' he said. 'The rooms were empty when I moved in.' He sounded regretful.

'And a rocking horse,' she said. 'Did you have a rocking horse when you were young?' and he shook his head.

They were all remembering long ago. They sat in silence for a moment, coffee cups in front of them, relaxed in a warm companionship. Janna had often sat like this with Andrew and Betsy, and Peter Craig slipped comfortably into the picture. In the soft candle-light she smiled at him, because he was looking at her and smiling.

Then the phone rang, making Janna jump, and Andrew got up, switching on the lights and dispelling the feeling that they could sit here for hours and nobody would disturb them.

'For you, Peter,' he said, holding the phone out to Craig. 'It's Harris.'

Another man got up, crossed the room, listened and then spoke. A man Janna hadn't met. She watched Peter Craig, her chin cupped in her hand, and the boyish face was as tough as any face she had ever seen. The voice was clipped and commanding. He only said a few words, but it was the other side of the coin, and she thought—how wrong can you be? He isn't a nice pleasant bloke. He's a Jekyll and Hyde.

'I'll be with you in a couple of hours,' he said, and replaced the receiver, and turned to tell them, 'I must be going.' He thanked them for the meal, said, 'It was nice meeting you,' to Janna.

She might have said, 'It was nice meeting both of

you,' but instead she smiled until he went on, 'Could you do me a meal for four on Saturday night?'

That stopped her smiling. No, she could not, but while she floundered for a convincing excuse—she couldn't pretend she was already booked, she'd announced this was her trial run—he said, 'Tonight's menu would do perfectly.'

'Hold on a minute,' she stammered, 'I don't know. I'm not sure that I am going to do it professionally after all—it was only an idea.'

Andrew answered for her. 'I'm sure she will.'

'Splendid,' said Peter. 'Eight o'clock all right?'

'Seems it will have to be,' shrugged Janna.

She turned on her two good friends the moment the front door of their apartment closed, demanding shrilly, 'Why did you let me in for that? You know I don't want to cook for him!'

'But I thought you did,' said Andrew, grin widening. 'Isn't this the new business venture? What are you going to call it—"Janna's Plaice and Chips"?' He winced at his own appalling pun, and Betsy said encouragingly,

'You could do it standing on your head. Dinner for four, that's no real trouble to you, is it? You've cooked for more than that many a time.' Before her father died Janna had had occasional buffet parties, supper parties. She hadn't done any entertaining since her father died, and Allan came. 'Of course you can do it,' Betsy insisted.

'But I don't *want* to go out cooking,' Janna yelped. 'And you knew that, didn't you?' She glared at the still grinning Andrew. 'You knew I'd got trapped in the kitchen and I was staying in there until he'd gone. *And* he knew. But I'll tell you something—it won't come cheap. He didn't ask what my terms were.'

'Don't make the bill too ridiculous,' said Andrew, sobering rapidly on a note of warning. 'Don't try to score off him.'

'What could he do?' she retorted. 'Sue me?'

They didn't want her getting on the wrong side of Peter Craig. His good will was very important to them, but she had been forced into this. He had taken advantage of her little white lie, and it would serve him right if Saturday's meal was an all-time flop.

She said grimly, 'He's a regular switch artist too, isn't he? The man on the phone was an eye-opener, a bit of a change from the man sitting here chatting us up over the coffee. Talk about Jekyll and Hyde!'

Andrew grinned again, but wryly this time. 'You think that was Hyde on the phone? That was Peter taking a business call. You should see him when he's really in action.'

'I hope I don't,' she said, emphatically. 'I don't think I'd enjoy it. I didn't particularly want to see him tonight, that's why I stopped in the kitchen. I'd be very happy not to be seeing him again, but it seems I've been conned into putting on a blessed dinner party for him on Saturday.'

# CHAPTER TWO

ALLAN stared as though she had taken leave of her senses when she told him next day that Peter Craig had booked her to produce a dinner for four on Saturday evening. 'He's got his nerve,' said Allan. 'I hope you told him you're nobody's skivvy.'

'I don't think he thinks I am,' said Janna. 'But I did cook last night's meal and there was some talk about me doing it professionally some time, and the next thing I knew I was taking this booking for Saturday.'

'I can't understand you,' said Allan. 'Letting yourself in for this.' He had walked over to the shop as soon as he got home from school. There were no customers in at the moment and Janna was putting the final touches to a small flower arrangement in an old Willow Pattern teapot on the windowsill. She got in the bit about Saturday right away, she had been fairly sure that Allan would disapprove.

She wasn't enthusiastic herself. If it hadn't been for Betsy and Andrew she would have been on the phone today, leaving a message for Peter Craig if she couldn't speak to him. But Betsy wanted her to do it, and he had said the same menu would be fine, and four was a modest number, she could surely cook for four. She would have to make it clear, though, that she had decided not to go on with the scheme, that this was her final appearance in strange kitchens.

She explained, 'I can't get out of it this time, but I'm not going to make a habit of it.'

'And I'd thought we might go out on Saturday night,' said Allan. 'I've been hard at it all week and I felt like a break.'

'Make it Sunday,' she said cheerfully, and Allan went off to think about that. Janna was an ideal girl for a creative artist, so sympathetic and understanding, and he didn't like the idea of her spending time with Peter Craig. She was attractive and Craig was a go-getter. Allan was wishing now that he had accepted last night's invitation and gone along himself to keep an eye on things . . .

'Who are the guests going to be?' Janna asked Betsy. 'Do you know?' It didn't matter to her who Peter Craig entertained, but she was a little curious, and Betsy said,

'A man called Oscar Laurence and his wife. He's head of a construction company and the firm handles all their legal business. I should think the other one will be Caroline.'

Caroline Colway was the girl most seen with Peter Craig out of office hours, and the one who used his apartment most, although Janna had never seen her. Betsy didn't talk much about her. It seemed that when she was here Caroline expected to be waited on, and regularly left a sinkful of washing up and general disorder. 'I'm paid to keep the place tidy,' Betsy had said, 'but I'm no lady's maid, and she lolls about like an old-time movie queen giving her orders if he isn't around. I hope he never marries her.'

'He never married any of the others, did he?' Janna had said, by way of comfort. Because Betsy had told her that his colleagues considered Peter Craig was a confirmed bachelor. But she could understand why he was interested in Caroline when she saw the photograph.

Friday evening she went up with Betsy into Craig's apartment, carrying the goodies for tomorrow's meal. There was nothing here to remind her of the old days. Even the staircase, leading up to what had been the nursery in the attics, had changed. Once it had been a rickety set of stairs, creaking underfoot, no handrail, but now it was a wide flight of open oak steps between panelled walls. The landing at the top was shut off by a door, and through the door everything was light and airy.

The main room had white-painted walls and Italian furniture, glass-topped tables and beautiful chairs, and green ceramic-tiled flooring. There was a modern painting, almost filling one wall, swirls of colour, mostly greens and blues. One of the little round tower windows was at a corner of this room, another could be glimpsed through an archway, where a round dining table was surrounded by rush-seated armchairs and a door led into the kitchen.

Janna felt quite at home in the kitchen, because it was almost a duplicate of Betsy's, except that this had a microwave oven, and lacked the personal touches, the mugs on the dresser, the clutter around. Betsy's kitchen looked lived-in, but this room was stark and shining as a magazine advert.

Janna put down her basket on the working surface where Betsy had already deposited the bag she was carrying. You were almost among the treetops when you looked out of this kitchen window, and Betsy was beckoning her back into the big room, saying, 'Come and look around.'

Janna had whistled on her way through. She wasn't sure she could relax in here, but it was mighty impressive. It told anyone who called that Peter Craig was a very successful man.

Betsy began to guide her around, and Janna made admiring murmurs. 'Mmm, yes, he does do himself proud, doesn't he?'

'This is the guest room,' said Betsy, 'and this is his room.'

In Peter Craig's room was the only photograph in the apartment. The room was in browns and oatmeal, and the photograph standing on a dressing table, that was part of the bedroom fittings filling the whole of one wall, was the most vivid thing in it. You had to look at the photograph as soon as you stepped into the room.

It showed a girl, wearing a yellow strip of bikini pants, several long thin golden chains and a broad gold bracelet lying on a beach of silver sand. Her skin was a flawless all-over tan, and her eyes were closed. She had a half smile, as though she was dreaming or remembering a lovely sexy interlude, and Janna asked, 'That's Caroline?'

'The same.' Betsy sniffed. 'She put it there herself the last time she was here. Making sure he doesn't forget her.'

Janna had to smile. 'I shouldn't think he's likely to! She isn't hiding much, is she?'

'Her father's something high-and-mighty in the City,' said Betsy, admitting as though she would rather not, 'I suppose she'd make a good enough wife for an ambitious man. She always looks fantastic, and I suppose she knows everybody who's anybody, but I don't like her. She chucks her weight about too much for me.'

'With Peter Craig?' Janna was surprised to hear it, and Betsy grinned.

'Not likely! She wouldn't get far if she did. With me she does, when he isn't around. She thinks I'm the village yokel.'

Janna prepared as much of tomorrow's meal as she could, and for a while Betsy stayed with her, but when Andrew was due home Betsy went down to give him his tea and Janna was alone.

When she came out of the kitchen she stood looking around. There was nothing left up here of the old vicarage, except the round tower windows. This could have been a stylish apartment anywhere. Expensive and modern and functional, no fussiness, no sloppy comfort. She couldn't see Punch and Judy around these rooms. They both liked rugs and chairs they could curl up on.

Central heating would keep this place warm in

winter, but there wasn't even a pretend fireplace. Betsy and Andrew had an electric fire with logs to sit by. That was the focal point in their living room, but where was the heart in this apartment?

She went to the window and looked down, and that was how she remembered it. The same pattern of buildings and open spaces. Her own cottage with the paddock behind. There had been chickens in the paddock when she was a child. Now there was old Freddy in his little shed for the night. It was beginning to get dark, but she could still see clearly enough for that.

She turned on a few lights. Now that she was up here she was immensely intrigued by what Peter Craig had made of it. She opened the door of his bedroom for a final look at Caroline, and wondered what she would look like with her clothes on.

'Fantastic,' Betsy had said, and with a figure like that she could hardly miss. It wouldn't matter to Janna whether she was friendly or not, because after tomorrow night Janna wouldn't be meeting her again.

Peter Craig wasn't cold fish all through, it seemed, although he probably chose his ladies with care. Miss Colway knew everybody who was anybody, and would make a good wife for an ambitious man, and they didn't come more ambitious than Peter Craig. Janna found it all rather distasteful. She would have liked him better if his girl-friend had been more ordinary.

She found herself walking slowly towards the photograph. While she was here Caroline shared this room, of course, the king-size bed, one of the fitted wardrobes. The articles on the dressing table were a man's: hairbrush and comb, leather stud box, an onyx ashtray; but there were drawers into which a girl could stack her cosmetics.

She slid back one of the wardrobe doors and on the hangers were several dresses. Possibly Miss Colway would wear one of these tomorrow night. Which one? Janna wondered idly. What was her favourite colour?

What colour were her eyes when they were open?

She heard a door open and froze, certain that Peter Craig was about to march in and find her rooting through his wardrobe. When she saw Betsy in the living room she sagged with relief and croaked, 'I'm in the bedroom.' As Betsy stepped in she said, 'Actually I'm in the wardrobe. Thank heavens it's you! What *should* I have said I was doing?'

Betsy grinned. 'Poking around, because you're nosey.'

'Aren't I just? One thing leads to another. I took another look at her photograph, then I found myself wondering what she'll be wearing tomorrow night.'

'What are you wearing?' asked Betsy.

'That won't matter, will it? Nobody will see me. But I don't think I'll come in jeans again.'

She put on a coral cotton shirtwaister, and Allan came across just as she was leaving to go over to the Old Vicarage. 'You're going through with it then?' he said, as though she was emigrating, and she laughed.

'I am only cooking them a meal.'

'What time will you be back?'

'I don't know.'

'No point in me waiting around for you?'

'You can if you like, of course. You could keep Punch company.'

'No, thank you,' said Allan quickly, and Punch seemed to feel the same way.

Betsy had laid the table for four, and put flowers around, and Janna carried on with the preparations for the meal. It was more or less the same as the one she had cooked at Betsy's, with slight variations to amuse herself. At Betsy's she had given them a melon and lime sorbet, tonight she produced melon crescents.

By a quarter to eight she had everything in hand, and she was almost wondering if it might not be fun to do this professionally sometimes. But you couldn't launch a business enterprise on a sometimes basis. It would mean you could only cook for people who knew you well, and you could hardly charge them. She hadn't the slightest idea what she should be charging Peter Craig. She would probably end up saying, 'I'll leave it to you, give me what you think it was worth.' He had paid, via Betsy, for the ingredients. More likely it would be, 'Have this one on the house, I've decided to stick to my amateur status.'

When he walked into the kitchen it took her a little by surprise because she hadn't heard anyone enter the flat. She was concentrating on her pots and pans, and singing softly to herself, and when the kitchen door opened she jumped. 'Oh, hello,' she said. 'Everything's coming on nicely.'

'Hello.' He was expensively clad, in a conservative suit, grey silk shirt, grey tie; and he gave her a smile that made her smile back, although she knew it was part of his stock in trade. The boyish grin hiding the razor mind.

Caroline was standing just behind him, eyeing Janna up and down, with an expression that brought back Betsy's words—'She thinks I'm the village yokel.' Janna almost started to laugh. Her lips were twitching when Peter introduced them, and she had to swallow before she could say steadily, 'How do you do?'

'Very well, thank you,' said Caroline coolly. 'And so it seems do you. Do you do much of this?'

She looked at the stove and the kitchen table as though the sight of a meal in preparation was astonishing.

'If you mean cooking,' said Janna, 'not often with a liqueur bottle. The Grand Marnier is strictly for occasions.'

She didn't care if she got on the wrong side of Caroline. She was a very temporary member of Peter Craig's staff, and nobody was going to put her down. 'Dinner at eight,' she said sweetly. 'If you'll just get out of the kitchen now.'

Caroline swished back, a few minutes later. She was wearing a dress in a style that Janna recognised. She had a couple from the same designer hanging on her racks, and she wondered what Miss Colway did with her clothes when she tired of them. But one look at Caroline warned her they weren't going to have that kind of discussion.

'Do you live in this funny little village?' Caroline drawled.

'Just up the road.'

Janna was cutting the half melons—with their rose pink filling of strawberry jellied melon and mandarin oranges and Grand Marnier—into three slices each. She operated the knife carefully and Caroline said, 'I've been wondering where on earth Peter found you. Are you hoping to cook for him regularly? He has one village girl who's supposed to keep the place clean, but cauliflower cheese seems to be about her limit in the kitchen.'

Cauliflower cheese and baked beans were two of Betsy's standbys. But Betsy wasn't employed to cook anyway, and Janna was deciding that she couldn't stand Caroline. She said, 'Do you mean Betsy? Her husband's one of Peter's articled clerks.'

'Really?' Caroline shrugged, indicating that if anyone had mentioned that to her before she had forgotten. 'Some men seem to marry the most unsuitable girls.'

'That they do,' Janna agreed. 'And how long have you and Peter been going around together?'

'About six months,' said Caroline, caught off balance. Then her lips tightened. 'But you won't be cooking for him again after tonight, so don't get any ideas.'

She thought that Janna had designs on Peter Craig, and that was funny; only Janna didn't feel like handing her a laugh. She would rather have given her something to worry about. It was a pity that Caroline was so elegant and so beautifully made up, while Janna was looking like the girl who had dropped by to help out in the kitchen.

No competition there, Caroline was probably telling herself. But when she brought up the subject later, that Janna might not be suitable as a permanent cook, and Peter explained that tonight's dinner was a one-time, she might feel rather a fool. Janna hoped she would.

Peter came into the kitchen, and Caroline hurried across to him to brush an invisible hair from his shoulder. Her long white fingers stayed, patting and fussing, telling Janna—this is mine, keep your hands off, and Peter said, 'You've only laid for four.'

He didn't seem to notice Caroline, fiddling with the lapel of his jacket. He was speaking to Janna and she said, 'That's right. You said four.'

'But you'll be eating with us.'

'Oh no!' she said, and Caroline said it too, chorusing the same words. Caroline went on, 'That would be most unsuitable,' and when Peter's eyebrows rose she said, 'Well, look at the girl! How she's dressed.'

He looked and grinned and asked, 'The pinafore is detachable, isn't it?'

'Oh yes,' said Janna. They were both laughing, because of course there was nothing wrong with her dress. She wouldn't have chosen it for a dinner party, but it was cool and clean and comfortable, and Peter said,

'We're not entertaining royalty.'

What Caroline meant was that she didn't want Janna eating with them, and neither did Janna. But when Peter went back into the dining area, to set another place, Caroline hissed, 'You'll only make a fool of yourself,' and that did it.

Janna had been going to stick by her refusal, but after that she said brightly, 'Oh, I'm sure somebody will tell me which fork to use,' and got a furious glare.

Betsy didn't get on with Caroline either, but this was more than snobbery. She really was going out of her way to be offensive. Having found Janna in Peter Craig's kitchen it seemed that Caroline actually did suspect her of planning to move into his bedroom. Highly insulting, thought Janna. If the first fifteen minutes were anything to go by this should be a lively evening!

As Peter placed another chair at the table the buzzer went. Somebody was ringing his bell down at the front door. 'That should be the Laurences,' said Caroline. He went to answer it, and before Caroline closed the kitchen door behind her she said, 'Stay in here,' as though she was addressing a troublesome puppy, and Janna was not sure how long this would continue to be amusing.

Caroline's appalling rudeness was beginning to irritate her. Much more of it and she would go further than the snappy reply, she would blow the scene wide open. She would tell Caroline Colway that Peter Craig was the last man she hankered to get into bed with, and that Caroline herself had worse manners than a fishwife—whatever a fishwife was. Well, something like that.

The sooner she dished up and got away the better. Betsy and Andrew had Punch downstairs in their apartment, Janna was joining them as soon as she was through in here, and she must remember every insulting gem that had fallen from Caroline's lips, so that she could repeat it all, and have them indignant at first maybe, but finally falling about with laughter.

Of course it was funny. Of *course* it was, and she put a few seconds' furious energy into whipping up the cream.

The first course was on the table. They would be talking and having drinks for a few minutes, and she wouldn't join them after all. She would be happier and safer in here; she wasn't looking for an open clash with

Caroline. That wouldn't go down too well with Peter, and Peter was Andrew's boss.

Peter came into the kitchen and invited, 'Come and be introduced.'

She went in her apron, she was the cook, and he didn't give her the chance to hang back. He held the door open for her, with his guests standing by the round window in the dining area, where they could see and hear him.

Oscar Laurence was a big smiling man in his fifties, and his wife was smiling too. She had the same golden tan as Caroline, and she wore a black dress, long-sleeved and scoop-necked, knife-pleated from the hips. She looked much younger than her husband, until you got close enough to see the faint skin lines here and there. But her figure was girlish, and it was vitality and enthusiasm more than cosmetics or money that were keeping her youthful.

Peter introduced Janna, adding that she was the girl who had prepared the meal, and Sylvia Laurence said that she loved cooking herself.

She and her husband were quite happy to accept Janna. It was Caroline who was hovering in the background with a worried frown, asking 'Who's going to do the serving if we're all sitting down?'

'What will you drink?' Peter asked Janna—one of the cabinets had opened on a variety of bottles—and she began to say,

'Oh, a bitter lemon,' when she changed her mind. 'A sherry, I think. Please.'

He poured her one, and she drank a little, then she said, 'Somebody should be in the kitchen.'

'Nonsense. Sit down, everyone,' said Peter, and Caroline seated the Laurences, acting the hostess, making quite a business of getting five people round a largish table. 'Take your apron off, then,' said Peter to Janna. 'Unless it's part of the outfit.'

She wasn't arguing out here, and the Laurences

seemed pleasant enough. She undid the tapes at her waist, but those fastened in a bow behind her neck were in a tangle, and as she fumbled Peter said, 'Here, let me.'

'I seem to have got it into a knot.' She wasn't nervous, but everyone was looking at her and somehow she had jerked the strings tighter. 'Ouch!' she exclaimed as her hair pulled.

'Stand still,' he said.

She ducked her head, and saw Caroline glaring at her. Oh lord, Caroline thought this was all part of a ploy. Although goodness knows what she imagined Janna hoped to get from Peter Craig undoing a knot in two tapes behind her.

But she could feel his fingers brushing against the nape of her neck, under her hair, and the light touch seemed to run right down her spinal column, sending a tingling sensation through every nerve in her body. As though he was running his hands over her, naked; the colour rose in her cheeks, and she put up her own hands to pull his away.

'If it's a tight knot break it. I can easily sew on another tape.'

The tapes slid apart and he said, 'Don't be so impatient.'

'Sorry.' She took the apron and dropped it on a kitchen chair. 'I do get impatient. Knots you can't undo are very annoying.' She was making a silly little joke, and the Laurences obligingly chuckled.

'Especially on presents,' said Sylvia Laurence. 'Especially when you can't find the scissors.' But Caroline didn't smile, and Peter said,

'We differ there. I'm a patient man.'

She wondered why he was telling her that. He seemed to be telling her, not Caroline nor the Laurences. He was still standing, looking at her, and her nerves were still raw from his touch as though their extra-sensitivity was warning her there was a dangerous message in what he had just said.

Or the sherry was stronger than she had realised. She took her seat and they started on the first course, and everyone but Caroline—and Peter who was having it for the second time in four days—was complimentary about the pâté.

Sylvia Laurence was a nice woman. She jumped up when the first course was finished, and insisted on going into the kitchen with Janna to dish up the main course.

Caroline didn't move, and when they settled down again Caroline guided the talk into channels that left Janna high and dry. She didn't know the people they were talking about, nor the places. So she sat quietly, eating her meal. Andrew was never going to join this club, not even when he had all his legal qualifications. Peter Craig would always be a high flyer, but Andrew and Betsy would have an ordinary life, and who was to say they wouldn't have more in solid assets—like happiness—to show for it at the end?

Hee-haw . . . Oscar Laurence was talking about the government's last ruling on tax laws, when suddenly over the quiet night air a donkey's bray reached them; and Sylvia threw back her head and laughed, 'What *is* that? Is that a *donkey*?'

'Oh, we have donkeys round here too,' said Peter. 'But they're the four-legged variety.'

'We have all sorts of noises round here,' said Caroline gaily. 'You expect city sounds, but things roar at you here in the dead of night, and scream and howl. It can be terrifying round here between dusk and dawn.'

Her smile rested on Peter, with the intimacy of shared memories. Janna had no doubt that she had been woken by strange country noises, and reached for him in that bed through that door, where her photograph was on the dressing table.

She said, 'That was Freddy.'

'They have names?' said Caroline.

'Of course,' said Janna. 'And he's mine—my old donkey.'

'What do you do with donkeys?' asked Caroline. 'They don't pull things, do they? Ploughs or carriages or anything. Do you *ride* them?'

'The village children do sometimes,' said Janna. 'But he's too old to do much but amble round the paddock.'

'What fun,' said Caroline, deadpan, and then with a burst of animation she began to talk about a cruise on the Laurences' yacht last Christmas, the four of them and others who sounded just as glamorous and just as rich.

'Now when are we going to do something like that again?' asked Caroline, leaning towards Peter with promise and pleading, as though it was up to him.

He said, 'I'm very busy these days,' and Oscar nodded—he was busy too, he understood.

'But any time you want to use the yacht,' he said to Peter, and Janna could imagine Caroline draped out in the sunshine improving her enviable tan. Sharing a cabin with Peter, of course.

All the time Caroline was emphasising her claims on Peter, her links with him. Never taking her eyes off him for more than a moment, touching him as often as she could. Betsy had said he was supposed to be a confirmed bachelor, but when Caroline said, 'Peter and I——' and she kept saying that, it came out with exactly the same inflection as, 'my husband and I'.

The meal was appreciated. It went down very well, and Janna drank two glasses of rosé wine, and felt quite pleased with herself.

She liked the Laurences. She thought Caroline was a pain in the neck and Peter Craig was a calculating charmer and nobody's fool. When Caroline reached her long pointed-nailed hand for him he smiled, but she wasn't holding him; Janna could have told her that. The cool blue eyes were amused, and if anyone was making a fool of herself tonight it was Caroline, not Janna.

When Janna got up to fetch the coffee Caroline said, with thinly disguised sarcasm, 'You won't mind if we leave the washing up, will you? We're going out.'

'Yes, of course,' said Janna.

'Aren't you coming with us?' Sylvia Laurence asked, and Peter added,

'Do come.'

It was months since Janna had been anywhere but the very occasional trip to the cinema. Her business, and Allan, had taken up almost all of her time, and Allan's idea of a night out was a meal in a local pub. That was all right, she always enjoyed herself, but suddenly she wanted to go wherever they were going.

'A cabaret,' said Peter. 'And dancing. Do you dance?'

'I used to,' she said, idiotically, like an ageing ballerina.

She had enjoyed dancing once in a while, and then after her father died Allan had become the man in her life, and Allan didn't dance. She asked, 'Do you?' and Peter grinned.

'Badly, but I need the exercise.'

'Do you have another dress?' said Caroline, and Janna bit back the words, 'A hundred and forty nine at the last count. I sell 'em.'

She said, 'Could you give me ten minutes?'

'Twenty,' said Peter.

'I'll be back,' she promised. 'Leave the washing up. I'll do it in the morning.'

She ran down the stairs to Betsy and Andrew's flat, and tapped smartly on the door. Betsy answered and Punch squirmed past her, and Janna stooped to pat the dog and ask, 'May I leave him, I've been invited to go on to some club with them?'

'Sure,' said Betsy.

'You go and have a night on the tiles,' said Andrew.

'Will you come and help me get ready?' Janna asked. 'I've got about fifteen minutes, and I want to go back looking as good as Caroline Colway, or better if possible.'

They ran all the way up the lane to Janna's Place, and went through the evening dresses like shoplifters, picking out the best at speed. 'Where are you going?' Betsy wanted to know.

'I don't know. Dancing and cabaret somewhere.'

'Who asked you? Peter, did he?' Betsy held Mrs Morrison-Jones' cream silk number at arms' length and put it on the oak chest for further inspection.

'Yes. I ate with them too. They're nice, the Laurences. But Caroline seems to have the idea that I'm after her feller. She thinks I'm there as his regular cook and she's mad about that.'

'Good,' said Betsy, with a happy smile. 'I hope it keeps her awake at nights.'

'She gives the impression that Peter does that,' said Janna drily, and as she spoke the words left an acrid taste in her mouth.

'How about this?' said Betsy.

The dress was a handful of silk, but when Janna slipped into it it took on the lines of her slim young body, not obviously, discreetly, suggestively, rippling and sensuous. It was green, the best colour for Janna, mid-calf length at the front and dipping at the back, echoing the cape collar, which dipped to a point at the back. A wickedly simple dress, from the same collection as the dress Caroline wore.

'Snap,' Janna could say. In any case Caroline would realise that this was a far cry from the little cotton number Janna had worn under her apron.

She stripped off her make-up as fast as she could, putting it on again, accenting her cheekbones and the wide pure curve of her mouth, while Betsy flicked a comb through her hair. She wanted to look the equal of Sylvia and Caroline, and she took along Mrs Morrison-Jones' velvet coat for good measure. It could be cool before she returned.

The change was a transformation. She looked as jet-set as either of them, striking and sophisticated, and Betsy stood back, hands on her hips, and said, 'You're fantastic. It's a shame you don't get yourself up like this more often. You always were the best-looking girl in the school.'

'Who wouldn't be, in this gear?' said Janna, and the clothes helped, of course. Janna was no raving beauty, but in clothes like these she could pass as one.

'Come and get an eyeful of this,' said Betsy when they reached her apartment. 'Back, Punch, you haven't been invited.'

Andrew stepped out on to the landing and goggled, 'It isn't Janna, is it?' Of course he knew it was Janna, but he was impressed although he was teasing. 'You want to watch it,' he said. 'Peter's due for a switch, according to the office grapevine.'

'What?' said Janna.

'Six months is his average,' explained Andrew. 'Then girls start getting ideas about getting married, and he's been going around with the gorgeous Miss Colway for just over six months, so like I tell you, he's due for a switch.'

'Wouldn't that be something?' said Betsy. 'Janna's about due for a switch too.'

'You,' said Janna, 'are a barmy pair. Lucky you found each other, nobody else would stand you.'

She walked up the next two flights of stairs. The apartment just above Betsy was occupied by a retired colonel and his wife. That was where the main staircase ended. The new stairs, the flight that had replaced the nursery stairs, led to Peter's flat, and she tapped on the door. Although it was probably open, she could probably have walked right in.

He opened it. He seemed even taller in that open doorway, and for a moment they looked at each other as though they were assessing, measuring up something. His brown hair waved slightly, curling crisply at the nape of his neck. His mouth lifted in a lopsided grin, then he said, 'That was a remarkable ten minutes.'

He was as impressed as Betsy and Andrew had been. More, because he had never seen her before, except casually dressed and with hardly any make-up beyond a touch of eye and lip colouring.

She enjoyed his reaction, almost as much as she enjoyed Caroline's expression when she recognised the style of the dress. Janna felt a surge of confidence, because wherever they were going she could hold her own now, and she said, 'I hope I haven't kept you waiting.'

'You haven't,' said Peter. 'You could have taken an hour and this would still be worth it.'

Oscar Laurence nodded smiling agreement, and Sylvia went off into the bathroom to retouch her own make-up. Caroline went into Peter's bedroom, and Janna looked through the kitchen door at the dishes piled on the table. 'Not in this dress,' she said. 'I meant that. That washing up will have to wait till morning.' She wasn't trying to operate the dishwasher in this dress.

The table was booked and they were ushered to it with a minimum of fuss. The hotel had been an old house standing by the river, but an immense dining-dancing-room with a glass wall overlooking the river had been built on. The river was spotlit and you watched and heard it, so near but with the glass between you so that it didn't seem quite real, almost like a film playing away out there.

They had timed their arrival for the cabaret, and Janna enjoyed every minute. It was ages since she had seen a live performance. She thought the comedian was hilarious, and the singer—a black girl with a haunting voice—stirred her deeply. If she hadn't been in such blasé company she would have had tears in her eyes. But not in front of Peter Craig and his friends. So she kept blinking, although she applauded enthusiastically.

They danced. She danced with Oscar. This man was probably a millionaire, but it was easy enough to talk to him. The wine and the admiration had added to her confidence, and she had the exhilaration of escape for a while. Allan was more demanding than her father had been. Her father had wanted her to enjoy herself, go about with her friends, but Allan was all her friends—well, all her men friends. He wanted her in her little cottage, a few minutes away from his. Or somewhere he could phone her from the callbox on the green, and from which he could collect her.

Tonight was a taste of luxury and she was enjoying it. Work again on Monday, but tonight was really fun.

She danced with Peter. 'Who would have thought it?' she said, looking up at him, his arms lightly around her, now touching her, now letting her go. But they were together, and when they moved apart they came back. She added, 'I really don't know what I'm doing here.'

'Enjoying yourself, I hope,' he said.

'Yes, I am.'

'So am I,' and as they passed the table she felt Caroline's eyes, sharp as twin points between her shoulder blades. But she had no intention of feeling guilty about Caroline, a girl well able to guard her own interests.

You could dance out of here, on to a patio. Janna hadn't realised that until she found that they were outside, under the stars, with the music reaching them, faint but clear like music in the mind.

The patio was edged by a low wall, and a shallow flight of steps led down to gardens on the river bank.

Peter stopped when they reached the wall and drew her, by the hand holding hers, to sit down beside him.

'About this teacher-cum-writer of yours,' he said.

'Allan?'

'How many do you have?'

'Only one.'

'Are you marrying him?'

She was watching the few dancers who had come out here, and the couples who were strolling together, arms around each other. It was a hard question to answer because she had never really thought about it. She supposed she loved Allan, and she supposed he loved her, but she had never seriously considered marrying him. Perhaps because he had never asked her.

She said, 'I don't know about that. He's got his book to finish, and my shop might not seem much to you, but I'd like to work it up into a really worthwhile business, and we're all right as we are. We haven't discussed marriage.'

She wouldn't have thought it was a matter he discussed much. She felt the night breeze on her cheek and thought it was his breath and turned, surprising a look in his eyes she couldn't fathom. She said, 'Betsy and Andrew are happy, but there don't seem to be many happy marriages these days.'

'In my business,' he said, 'you see more failures than successes.'

Divorces. Settlements. Fights over property, money, children. She asked, 'Is that why you never married?'

'One very good reason.'

He was all the other reasons, she felt. The man he was. By now he must have chosen his way of life, with the calculation he brought to the legal problems he dealt with daily. He was not a man to be frightened of loneliness and no woman was going to hold him as Caroline wanted to hold him.

Allan was a dependent man, and Janna was lucky to be

needed. She liked being needed. Peter Craig would
never need anyone.

The music had finished and the dancers were wandering back into the bright lights of the hotel. 'Shouldn't
we be joining the others?' said Janna, and he held out a
hand to help her stand up. Then, when she was standing,
he looked at her face in the half light and stooped and
kissed her lips.

She knew, a few seconds before, that he was going to
kiss her, and everything stopped. It was a moment
without breathing, without feeling. His lips were light, he
only held her hand and the kiss seemed a token touch too.

She didn't move at all, but the tingling that had run
down her spine when he brushed the nape of her neck
was starting again. Like electricity. Like music inside
her. She heard music, although the music had stopped,
and she might have reached for him if she hadn't
pulled herself together.

She said, 'I've had a very pleasant evening,' mumbling
the words against his mouth, and he raised his head and
smiled.

'I'm delighted to hear that. Your lipstick is as delicious
as your cooking.'

'Was that what you were doing, tasting me?'

'Given the opportunity,' he said, 'I could make a
banquet of you.'

'I could give you indigestion.'

She was glad they were talking nonsense and she
could laugh, because she was finding Peter Craig
disturbing, and she was glad to get back inside where
the crowds were.

The other three were still at their table, and Janna's
cheeks flushed because of the way they looked at her.
The Laurences hid smiles, and Caroline said shrilly,
'We were wondering if we'd lost the pair of you.'

'It's a beautiful night,' Janna babbled. 'And it's
cooler outside.'

'*Cooler?*' Caroline's voice rose so that several people nearby began to take an interest. 'You don't look cooler. You look very overheated. What has Peter been saying to you? Or doing to you?'

Peter held out a chair for Janna, then sat down himself and said very quietly, 'That's enough.'

'Don't tell me what's enough,' snapped Caroline, with head-tossing petulance. She had probably never been thwarted before in all her life, and Janna was horrified to find herself at the centre of this kerfuffle.

'Excuse me,' she said, and fled for the Ladies. What with the music and the dancing, and one thing and the other, she didn't feel calm enough to make any useful contribution towards restoring the peace.

She didn't think Peter would allow Caroline to make a scene. He wouldn't have his clients—the Laurences—embarrassed. But she was embarrassed. She stared at herself in the long mirrored panel and her face was flaming. She ran the cold water tap over her fingertips, and dabbed her forehead and temples, then ran it over her wrists.

After that she did some deep breathing, and practised a serene expression. Sylvia Laurence came in when she was just about ready to go back, and said, 'Oh, dear me!'

'What's happening?' asked Janna.

'Caroline's booked herself in here for the night.'

'Here?'

'This is where we're staying.' Sylvia began to smile mischievously. 'We're leaving early in the morning, and we shall be having breakfast in our room, so with luck we shan't bump into her.' As Janna bit her lip she said, 'Cheer up, child. My husband was only saying yesterday that she was getting too possessive. He said the days of that affair were numbered.'

Janna had thought so herself, but she was glad to have it confirmed. As her face cleared Sylvia asked curiously,

'Are you and Peter seeing much of each other?'

'Oh no, we hardly know each other. I cooked a meal for some friends he was eating with earlier in the week, and he asked me to do tonight's meal. That was the first time we'd met.'

'Well, you did him a good turn tonight,' said Sylvia. 'You got rid of Caroline for him.' She beamed as though that was clever of somebody, and it had been quick thinking on the part of Peter Craig.

Caroline was jealous of Janna before she even set eyes on her. She would hardly have come into the kitchen as though she was meeting a rival unless Peter had already put the idea into her head. And then he had insisted Janna joined them, both for dinner and after. He had flirted with her, danced with her, gone out under the stars with her.

'Getting too possessive,' Oscar had said. 'Time for a switch,' Andy had said. And Janna had got rid of Caroline for him. He had used the situation, used her. She had danced for him like a puppet on a string.

Another couple of women came into the Ladies, and Sylvia Laurence touched Janna's arm to get her attention for a whisper of advice. 'We're very fond of Peter, but I wouldn't like a daughter of mine to fall for him. He's a hard man.'

She hadn't had much sympathy for Caroline, but she had seen something in Janna that reminded her of herself when young. 'Don't get too fond of him,' she added softly, and Janna said with all the ringing certainty in the world,

'Oh, I won't, I promise you. The more I hear about him the less risk there is of that.'

# CHAPTER THREE

THERE were only the men sitting at the table when Janna and Sylvia went back. They were talking, and as the Laurences didn't seem to like Caroline very much, Oscar had probably been congratulating Peter on getting rid of her.

Janna was finding it hard to contain her indignation. If the Laurences hadn't been around she would have given Peter Craig a blistering couple of minutes. As it was she held back the angry words and said coolly, 'I'd like to go home now. Would you mind phoning for a taxi for me?'

'I've called one,' said Peter. They had all come in the Laurences' car and she would have preferred leaving alone, but as they both went the same way home she could hardly insist on separate taxis.

Sylvia sat down again and, reluctantly, so did Janna.

'You will excuse us?' Oscar asked. They were discussing business so that for the next five minutes Sylvia and Janna talked together, and although Janna was seething she hid it well enough.

As a salesgirl she had had practice in hiding her feelings. All customers weren't amiable, you had to force a smile dealing with some of them; and this was easier because she liked Sylvia Laurence. By concentrating on her, and shutting off Peter, Janna had a cosy conversation about Sylvia's family—two sons and three grandchildren. When a waiter came across to say that the taxi had arrived the Laurences seemed sorry to see them go.

Nobody had mentioned Caroline. She must not only have booked a room but gone straight up to it, without toothbrush or night attire, and that dress was going to look out of place for breakfast.

The men would have realised that Sylvia had been telling Janna that Caroline had decided she wasn't going home with Peter, and as the taxi drew away from the hotel Janna said furiously, 'You set me up. You've been using me to make Caroline jealous!'

He closed the panel dividing them from the driver, then leaned back in his seat. 'That was a bonus,' he said cheerfully. 'You were hired to cook.'

Perhaps, but he had used the situation to anger Caroline and precipitate a public breach. That wasn't kind, but then he wasn't kind. 'Couldn't you have told the girl you were tired of her?' she demanded, and he said,

'I wasn't, until she began discussing honeymoons.'

Janna kept well to her own side of the seat, she didn't want to even brush against him. 'I don't think much of her taste in husbands,' she said tartly. 'You strike me as a rotten matrimonial risk.'

'Exactly.' He couldn't have agreed more.

'And she couldn't have cared much or she wouldn't have walked off so fast. It looks as though she was just waiting for an excuse.'

'Very likely,' he agreed again.

'Well, haven't you both had the lucky escape?' she said in acid tones, and turned her back on him, deliberately ending the conversation, staring through the window into the darkness, broken only by a very occasional street lamp or house light.

The journey was less than a quarter of an hour in all, but she was glad to reach the outskirts of the village. She was finding the cab claustrophobic. As he began to give the driver directions to Janna's Place she said, 'Just a minute.' Then she hesitated, changing her mind. 'That's it—yes, I do want to go straight home. I left my dog with Andy and Betsy, but it's too late to disturb them now, so I'll fetch him in the morning.'

Peter looked at her quizzically. 'For a moment I thought you were going to come up for a coffee.'

'You're joking,' she said. 'Goodnight,' she said, as the taxi drew up outside her front door. 'Such an interesting evening.'

'I thought so.' He was smiling, and well he might. If she had suspected what was behind his invitation that she should join them tonight she would never have come back here and got herself up to kill. Although she had enjoyed dressing up. She dressed up every working day in smart day clothes. But not romantically, not in the dreamier dresses.

Most of the evening had been enjoyable, the company, the cabaret, the dancing. Most of it until she had realised why she was out under the moon, being kissed by Peter Craig.

He had probably expected Caroline to follow them, to see the kiss. Fleeting though it was it could have had an explosive effect on Caroline. She would probably have stormed across and slapped both their faces—his first, with any luck. That would have given Janna a chance to duck, but it would have been horribly embarrassing.

Janna wasn't used to high-voltage emotional scenes. Peter Craig must handle them every day, and it was hard to imagine Caroline worrying about what on-lookers might be thinking, but Janna would have curled up in shame. It had been bad enough at the table, Caroline's shrill voice turning heads as everybody around decided this party could be more fascinating than their own.

She got out of her dress and took off her make-up. That was another thing Caroline would find awkward in the morning, no make-up, except whatever she carried in her purse. Perhaps she would hunt out Sylvia and borrow some. Lucky they both had lovely tans, but with an age gap of nearly twenty years it was unlikely they used the same products.

She covered the budgerigar, who opened one eye on his perch when the kitchen light came on, and croaked 'Wha-ha!'. The few words he had were in a strong Scottish accent, and nobody around here was Scottish. After Janna rescued him from her windowsill she had put a notice in the local paper and post office for a couple of weeks, with no takers. She had had him for the best part of a year, and although he fed heartily he still looked bedraggled.

Judy the cat purred, rubbing around Janna's ankles, drank a saucer of milk and curled up on her cushion on an old wickerwork armchair in the kitchen.

Janna missed Punch. He slept at the foot of her bed, and he was someone to talk to when the rest of the world was shut out. During the day doors were open and there were friends around. It was last thing at night when the doors were bolted that she talked most to Punch, and admitted her loneliness.

Tonight, when Peter Craig had asked her if she would be marrying Allan, it had been hard to answer. Maybe, she thought, lying under her patchwork quilt, with her arms folded under her head, and her dark hair flowing over the pillow. If Allan asked her, if she decided he was the man whose arms she wanted around her in the night.

Caroline wouldn't be reaching for Peter if any strange country sounds woke her up tonight, and somehow that made Janna smile.

Perhaps the test was bolting the door, and feeling complete with whoever was locked in with you. It probably would be Allan, but before then she would have to have a long serious talk with Punch, and assure him that Allan was on their side. She laughed in the darkness, imagining herself doing that.

Next morning was Sunday, and when she woke at the usual time—around eight o'clock—it was lovely to snuggle down again for an extra half hour. She might have made it longer, except that Punch would be causing trouble for Betsy and Andy, insisting on being let out when they had no garden to open the door and shoo him into. They would have to dress, and take him downstairs.

She put on jeans and a lightweight sweater, and was brushing her hair when she heard Punch bark. He had got them up, and one of them was probably returning him although he would have trotted home happily enough on his own. Janna knelt on her bed to push up the latch and push open the dormer window, and the white muslin curtain blew across her face, so that she thought the man coming up the lane with Punch was Andy.

'Sorry,' she began, and then, when she leaned out and recognised Peter Craig—who didn't look in the least like Andy, 'That's my dog.'

'I haven't kidnapped him,' he called back.

She had been so astounded she had sounded accusing. Now she scrambled off the bed and hurried downstairs, opening the house door, asking—still surprised, 'Did they ask you to bring him back?'

'I offered,' he said. 'We didn't settle up last night.'

Of course she was supposed to have been cooking professionally, and somehow she didn't feel too happy about that. She wouldn't have sent in a bill if he hadn't come round, and there was no need to turn up at this hour as though she was desperate for her cash. 'Come in,' she said as Punch jumped practically into her arms. 'All right, all *right*!' she exclaimed. 'I was just coming for you.'

Peter was looking round her living room, although this wasn't his kind of place. There was nothing in the furnishing line to interest anybody—comfortable cottage stuff. Her father's paintings were the only pictures, and his gaze rested on a study from the hills, when the golden wheat was growing in the fields below. She told him, 'My father painted them.'

'Very attractive,' he said, and that meant nothing, although it was an attractive scene, dappled with late afternoon sunshine. She would always be able to look at that picture and remember the sunny day he had started to paint it.

'What do I owe you?' Peter Craig was asking.

He had taken out his cheque book and she had to admit, 'I don't know. I never cooked for a fee before.'

He raised an eyebrow, and of course she would have found out what to charge before embarking on a part-time catering career. He used the sideboard to rest the chequebook on, and handed the cheque to her. 'I think you'll find that compares favourably with the going rate.'

Not bad at all, she thought, and watched herself tear the slip of paper across. 'Forget it,' she said. 'I had a good dinner and a very instructive evening. Besides, I've no plans to cook professionally. I was helping Betsy, and I got stuck in the kitchen, because you arrived early and I didn't want to come out and meet you.'

'You have something against me?' He didn't sound surprised, and there must be men and women who blamed him for their ruined lives. Clients, when judgment went against them. Others whom he had opposed. There must be plenty who hated a lawyer like him, but it hadn't been personal for Janna, and she explained,

'I didn't like the sound of you, that's all. Andy admires you tremendously, you're the man he'd most like to be like, though he never will. But from what I've heard of you you're too calculating and cold-blooded for my tastes, so I was keeping out of your way.'

'Cold-blooded?' Peter sounded as though he couldn't believe his ears. Last night he had kissed her, and that had been warning enough that he could be a very expert lover, but it didn't mean he wasn't cold-blooded.

'And calculating,' she said. 'I tried to spare everybody's feelings on Tuesday, but after the way you played me off against Caroline I was right in the first place. I should have said goodbye as soon as Andy yanked me out of the kitchen.'

'I'm glad you didn't.'

'Of course you are. I cooked your meal *and* I got you off the hook.'

'What are you doing today?' That made her blink, but her plans wouldn't include him and she said frostily, 'Why?'

'If you won't let me pay for the meal you cooked will you let me take you out?'

'*No!*' she said sharply.

'Why not?'

For the reason she hadn't wanted to meet him in the first place. Because they had nothing to say to each other. They were worlds apart. It was obvious to her, and she had just told him so in blunt language. She said, 'You don't get the message, do you?'

'I do,' he said quietly, 'but I'm not sure that you do.'

She suddenly tensed as if he was coming closer. The space between them seemed less. Peter had a powerful personality; she could see him dominating the opposition, influencing the audience, but he wasn't going to influence her. If he had a few spare hours today he could find another girl to keep him company. He shouldn't have been so hasty unloading Caroline.

Through the open kitchen door the budgerigar, woken by their voices although the cover was still on its cage, announced in muffled tones, 'It's a braw mornin'.'

'McNaught,' Janna explained gravely. 'My budgie.'

'Is that so?' he said, equally gravely. 'I thought you had a Scotsman in a cupboard.'

She took off the cover, revealing the ruffled little bird. 'He's healthy enough,' she said. 'He'd lost most of his feathers when he landed on my windowsill, but I don't think he's ever been a champion.'

She opened the door for the cat, who stretched and then walked with dainty fastidious steps into the garden. 'A braw mornin',' McNaught told them again.

'He came talking like this,' she said. 'And nobody around here seemed to have lost him, so perhaps he is from north of the Border. If he is it was a long trip.'

'If he is he's a champion,' said Peter. 'You've got a small menagerie here.'

'They're company.' She hadn't meant to sound defensive. She wouldn't like him to think she was lonely. She said, 'Nobody else wanted them,' and she need not have told him that either, sounding as though she was running a home for waifs and strays.

The garden gate clicked and Allan appeared round the side of the house. Punch growled, not savagely but unwelcoming, and Peter looked enquiringly at Janna. 'It's Allan,' she said.

'Your dog doesn't like him.'

'At times,' she said, 'my dog can be a bit thick.'

Allan saw her in the doorway and called, 'Good morning,' took another couple of paces and saw Peter just behind her. His face fell, the smile wiped off it. He didn't know who this man was, but he was taller and bigger than Allan; dressed as casually but with something about him that confused Allan, who was almost sure he was Peter Craig, and about the last man Allan wanted in Janna's kitchen this time in the morning.

She introduced them while Allan was still walking. When he stepped into the kitchen there was no table laid, no smell of coffee, no make-up on Janna's face. Peter Craig looked shaved and spruce, but Janna's appearance was that of a girl who hasn't been up long.

'What time did you get through last night?' Allan asked her.

'About midnight.' She wasn't sure of the exact time. She glanced at Peter, and he nodded confirmation, and Allan asked,

'What's this, then?' meaning what was Peter doing here.

Peter shrugged, and Janna explained, 'Peter brought Punch back. From Betsy's.'

Punch wouldn't have walked with Allan; he couldn't have taken Punch anywhere. She hadn't thought about that before, but she presumed Allan was thinking about it now, and scowling a little. 'Are you staying?' Allan asked truculently.

Janna had never seen any sign of jealousy in him before. Of course she had never given him any cause for jealousy. He had walked into a void in her life, and from then on there had only been Allan.

Peter seemed to be waiting for her to answer and she said, 'No, he is not staying.'

'Goodbye, then,' said Peter, as though the decision was hers. He wrote out the cheque again, leaving it on the kitchen table. 'Thank you,' he said, 'for an excellent meal.'

'Thank you,' she said. She couldn't tear it up all over again, without Allan wanting to know the reason, so she left it lying there.

He went out the way Allan had come in, across the little garden patch, round the side of the house, through the garden gate, and Allan commented, 'He's in a hurry to settle his debts, isn't he?'

'What's wrong with that?' Janna demanded, and began to fill the kettle. 'Have you had any breakfast?'

'Just coffee. Do you like him?'

'Not much.' She lit the gas and put the kettle on the ring.

'He likes you,' said Allan. 'He'd have stayed for breakfast.'

She moved around the kitchen, laying the table. She wasn't hungry, but she would feed Allan. 'Did he stay the night?' said Allan.

'I've told you what he was doing here.'

'Have you?' There was disbelief in his voice and her face grew hot. Her flesh warmed as she thought—yes, he likes me. If I'd gone back to his apartment he would have tried to make love to me. I wonder how it would have been, letting him love me.

She hadn't felt this kind of curiosity for a long time; she wasn't sure that she ever had. She was pretty, a warm and winning girl, she had had her admiring pursuers. But since her father died there had only been Allan, and Allan was not surprising.

None of the men she had known had been surprising. They had been nice enough, or she wouldn't have had them as friends, but she had never gone crazy for any of them. Not that there was any risk of her flipping over Peter Craig, but he was clever, brilliant. He'd be a stimulating companion and a stimulating lover. There was so much about him that she didn't know, and never would.

'I'm not going to quarrel with you,' said Allan.

He must have read indignation in the set of her shoulders. Janna hadn't turned round. She had been at the kitchen cupboard, taking out a pot of marmalade, when Allan asked if Peter had slept with her, and she was still standing with her back to him, holding the marmalade.

He must have thought she was frozen with fury. It would have shocked him if she had explained that she had been wondering how the night would have gone if his suspicions had been correct.

She said, 'Go home and get your own breakfast.'

She wasn't angry. She was acting outrage because it should have been a natural reaction, and because suddenly she didn't want Allan sitting here, waiting for bacon and eggs to be cooked.

'Very well,' he shrugged, looking hurt as a rebuffed child.

He wanted her to say again that she had slept alone

last night, and repeat that she didn't much like Peter Craig, but she had given him all the reassurance he was getting, and she didn't want to spend the rest of the day with Allan.

That was a change. Allan had seemed a part of her life that might go on for ever. It was as though she had been travelling down a straight road, and then suddenly reached a parting of the ways, faced with the dilemma of which path to take.

'You know where to find me,' said Allan. He wasn't sure what had happened, but as soon as he calmed down he would remember that Janna would never invite a stranger to stay the night. It would be completely out of character for her, and he had been stupid to suggest that she had. But Peter Craig had thrown him, standing by her as though Allan was disturbing something. There had been something in the way the man had looked at her and in the sharpness of her voice. They had been very aware of each other, those two.

If Janna didn't turn up at his house by midday he'd go back to hers. Besides, she always cooked Sunday lunch; Allan didn't keep much food in the house.

Janna turned out the gas under the kettle, and went to let Freddy out of his shed and walk around the paddock with him, Punch at her heels. Dogs and donkeys are supposed to be traditional enemies, but Punch and old Freddy got on well enough.

In the kitchen the cheque was still lying on the table. Janna thought they had settled that. She didn't want it. She would ask Betsy to leave it in Peter's apartment because she didn't expect to see him again. She didn't want Peter Craig disrupting her life. She knew that Allan expected her to follow him, and perhaps later in the day she would go over and make the peace.

She spent a few minutes putting on a modicum of make-up, then folded up the cheque and slipped it into her hip pocket, and walked over towards the Old Vicarage.

The bells were chiming now for the early morning service. Janna was a fairly regular churchgoer; she had been all her life, born and bred so close to the old church. It was an old church. 'God Bless Our Sovereign Queen Elizabeth' had been painted over the arch of the altar in the year Elizabeth Tudor came to the throne; and there was a tomb, famous for brass rubbings, of a Lady Eleanor, 1530 to 1605, whose piety was proclaimed in a long poem, but who was still referred to locally as Nell the Witch.

Janna walked past the cars that were parked on the gravelled space between the church and the new vicarage. There was a taxi among them this morning, she wondered who that had brought.

The heavy front door of the Old Vicarage was open and as she climbed the dark oak-carved staircase she thought that perhaps she would return the cheque herself. Perhaps it wasn't fair to involve Betsy. She would knock on Peter Craig's door and say, 'I told you I wasn't for hire. You're wasting a lot of cheques this way.'

But as she reached Betsy's door it was flung open. 'I saw you coming,' said Betsy, 'I can't wait to hear——' and Janna was bundled into the flat, as though eavesdroppers were everywhere. 'He came and fetched Punch,' said Betsy, once they were safe inside, 'so he was anxious to see you again, wasn't he? He wasn't wasting any time.'

'He wanted to pay me,' said Janna, and Betsy grinned. 'That could have waited, couldn't it? He wanted to see you, didn't he? Come on.' She led the way into the kitchen, where Andrew was eating toast, still in his pyjamas. 'What happened?' She poured another cup of coffee and sat down, picking up her own half empty cup, waiting for Janna to take a place at the little kitchen table too. 'Did you enjoy yourself last night?'

'Yes.' Janna sat down. She could do with a drink. 'Hello,' she said to Andrew, who said,

'Carry on, don't bother about me.'

'Don't think he isn't dying to hear,' said Betsy. 'How did Caroline like your dress?'

'Not so much,' said Janna. 'She didn't like me either. She didn't come back here last night. After Peter danced with me she booked herself into the hotel and flounced off.'

It wasn't a secret. It had been altogether too public for Janna's tastes, but it stopped Betsy drinking her coffee, and it made Andy nearly choke on a piece of toast. 'You mean there was a scene?' said Andy when he finally got the toast down. That bothered him, though it hadn't bothered his boss, and Janna said mischievously,

'I'm afraid there was. When we came back to the table after the dance—we'd been dancing outside, in the dark, where nobody could see us—there was quite a scene. I wasn't in on the end of it because I withdrew to the loo, but Sylvia Laurence came and told me that Caroline had booked a room and gone up to it, and that was the last we saw of Caroline.'

'Oh, *goody*!' grinned Betsy.

Andrew was less enthusiastic. In spite of what he had said about Peter Craig being due for a change he would never have expected the glamorous Miss Colway to worry about Janna. Janna was a smashing girl, but he wouldn't have thought she was Peter's type, and the Laurence account was an important one. He hoped the Laurences hadn't been embarrassed. He asked, 'Were the Laurences there? Oh yes, you said Sylvia told you. How did they—I mean——'

'Like you,' said Janna, 'they said Peter and Caroline were through.' She was fooling now, teasing him. 'All in all,' she told him, 'I had me quite a time.'

Andrew coughed again, perhaps there was another crumb in his throat. Then he said, 'Look, Jan, about Peter, I wouldn't read too much into last night if I were you. Caroline Colway is a bit like that—temperamental. She's upper crust and she's always been pampered, and Peter's a born bachelor anyway. If they had a row last night I don't suppose you were the real cause of it.'

'Don't you?' She made a mock crestfallen face. 'And I thought it was my fatal fascination! I thought I had your Mr Craig right here.' She closed her fingers over the palm of her hand, and Andrew looked bewildered while Betsy was smiling.

'She's joking, you idiot,' said Betsy. 'All right, what did happen? Did Caroline really storm out?'

'She did that,' said Janna. 'She came into the kitchen looking for a row, and that's how it went all evening. She'd have picked one if he'd danced with a bearded lady. Mind you, I think he set me up to make her walk out on him.'

'Let's hope she doesn't change her mind,' said Betsy, and touched the back of her wooden chair.

Perhaps if Betsy had come to the door with her Janna wouldn't have gone up to Peter's apartment. She might have handed over the cheque and asked Betsy to return it, or she might have torn it up again. But after she'd drunk her coffee they were still finishing their breakfasts, so she said goodbye for now, and let herself out.

She stood irresolute, looking up the stairs, and Punch waited. Then she shrugged and ran lightly up the two flights, to the door at the top, and tapped on it before she had time to change her mind.

Punch had never been up here before, and the top flight of open-plan steps needed careful negotiation. He was only half way up when Peter opened the door.

Peter's smile was slight, but it lingered in his eyes,

and Janna thought—he knew I'd come. Somehow that didn't annoy her too much. 'Come in,' he invited, and although she could have given him the cheque right there she went past him, into his apartment, and he held the door open the few moments longer it took for Punch to get to the top.

Then she said, 'Don't you ever listen to what people say?'

'Every day,' he said.

'Don't you ever believe they mean what they say?'

'Very rarely.'

Of course you couldn't believe all you were told if you were a lawyer, and she said, 'That might apply to the folk you meet professionally, but I do say what I mean, and I don't want to be paid for cooking that meal.'

'That leaves me in your debt.' And why not, for such a small matter? Why did he have to be so independent?

'Why not?' she said. 'I might need a lawyer some day.'

'I hope not.' His smile did something warming to her heart that made her smile too.

'So do I.' She took out the cheque from her back pocket. 'How much of your time would this buy me?'

'About five minutes on the open market.'

'Are you in it just for the money?'

'Would you believe me if I said I wasn't?'

Janna was surprised to find how much she wanted to believe that the ambition and the ruthlessness were tempered by caring. But she knew his reputation, and no one ever said he was a gentle man.

Punch began to explore. The ceramic-tiled floor and the spacious cool of the apartment had thrown him at first; he was used to small, cosy, cluttered rooms. He had stood just inside the door, nose twitching, while they were talking, but now he ventured towards a large armchair, in dark green velvet, and began to sniff all around it.

He was house-trained and well-behaved usually, but Janna was just about to remind him that this was not the great outdoors. 'Punch——' she began, on a warning note, when the main bedroom door opened and Caroline came out.

She wore a blue silk suit, and her hair was tied back with a matching scarf. She carried a suitcase, and when she saw Janna she went right on walking. 'What did you leave behind last night?' she said.

So this was why he'd wanted Janna round. And here she was—how about that for timing? He knew Caroline would arrive to collect her things, and he hoped that Janna would return with the cheque. As Caroline walked by Janna would have stepped forward, made some sort of protest maybe, but Peter held her arm and the feel of his fingers on her skin, even through the stuff of her sleeve, seemed to take her strength away.

'Goodbye, Peter,' said Caroline at the door. 'Look after yourself.'

She gave a hoot of mirthless laughter. 'That's a damn stupid thing to say when you always do.' She shut the door with a slam. That must have been Caroline's taxi among the cars outside the church.

'Sorry about that,' said Peter, and Janna said coldly, 'Any little thing I can do to help.'

He hadn't even offered to carry the case. It wasn't heavy, Caroline had been carrying it easily, and she would almost certainly have refused to let him touch it, but he might have offered. Janna's eyes were stinging as though the atmosphere had become filled with fumes and her throat had tightened. She said, 'So this is why you came round early to try to book me up for the day?'

'What?' A small frown cut between his brows.

'Was she here when you brought Punch back?'

'She arrived ten minutes ago.'

'You were expecting her, of course?'

'Not quite this early.'

They were still standing, a few paces inside the room. Peter touched her arm again and she moved away from him into the green velvet armchair. She didn't want to sit down or stay, but somehow she was sitting down and he was in a chrome chair with padded sling seat, facing her across a table like a glass chrome-edged box.

She was sitting, and waiting to hear what he had to say. He said, 'Let's get this clear. I'm sorry about last night too, I realise it wasn't pleasant for you, but Caroline would have been walking out on me any day now without your help. You had very little to do with it.'

'You mean her six months were up?' His eyebrows raised, and because she was annoyed enough to be indiscreet she went on, 'That's how long your girl-friends usually last, isn't it?'

After a moment he said, 'Andrew?' Janna wished she could deny that, but he'd know that the gossip she'd heard about him had come through Andrew, and after another short pause Peter said, 'That's about it. After about six months they start asking which comes first, the job or them, and it has to be the job.'

He sat leaning forward, hands clasped loosely. His hands looked strong, the nails cut short, the thumbnails square. Janna rubbed her upper arm where his fingers had held her, without force or any real pressure, but she could still feel them there.

'I don't have the kind of time to spare that the average woman expects from a man,' he said. His grin was wry, admitting his failings and his priorities. Women, he was saying, tired of taking second place; but Caroline had seemed ready to marry him, even if the relationship was rocky.

Janna said, 'I thought you said Caroline was talking of honeymoons.'

'Caroline thought marriage might help. It wouldn't have done.'

If he wouldn't spare enough time for a girl-friend

he'd hardly dance attendance on a wife, and she said ironically, 'As I think I mentioned, you strike me as a rotten matrimonial risk,' and he burst out laughing.

'As you also said—Caroline must have known it too, or she wouldn't have been so quick to walk out.'

She nodded, eyes dancing. 'So you're in something of a quandary.'

'You mean I'm never going to find a woman who doesn't need more time than I can afford?'

It was a long way back in the green armchair. She couldn't lean back without overbalancing, so she leaned against the arm, smiling across at him. 'You haven't found one yet, have you?'

'No,' he admitted cheerfully. Of course he could find one. There were plenty of girls who would settle for what he had to offer. He was rich and successful and a charmer. 'How about you?' he asked. 'This school-teacher of yours that your dog doesn't like. How much of your time does he take up?'

That wasn't his business, but then Caroline wasn't her business and they had just been discussing Caroline. 'He likes me around,' she shrugged.

'How about today?'

'Today,' she said lightly, 'he's waiting for me to apologise.'

'Apologise for what?' and when she said,

'He isn't sure you came over this morning,' he chuckled,

'The suspicious type.'

'Not usually.' She and Allan had never quarrelled. 'Not that he's ever had any reason to be jealous,' she was almost thinking aloud. 'I don't meet many men these days. Mine's a female clientele, and I've only been around with Allan since——' Since her father died, but she changed that to, 'For quite a while.' Peter didn't say anything. 'I used to have other men friends,' she said, 'but now there's just Allan.'

'No,' he said, 'now there's Allan and me. You need another man around, from time to time.'

'What *are* you suggesting?' But he looked serious and when he wasn't smiling it was a thoughtful face.

'As a friend,' he said.

A little while ago Janna had thought they inhabited different worlds. Now she thought—why shouldn't we be friends? and she said, 'You could be right.'

'Don't apologise today.' There was entreaty in his voice. 'Spend today with me.'

'Where?' ·

'Anywhere.' He looked around. 'What's wrong with here for lunch?'

'Am I cooking again?'

She would enjoy having lunch up here, preparing another meal in the kitchen. 'There's food in the freezer,' he told her, 'and a microwave oven.'

'I've never used a microwave.'

She went to take another look at it, and opened the freezer lid and peered in. Yesterday she had brought fresh food, but there was a fair stock of ready prepared in here. 'You could last out a short siege,' she commented.

'Shall we bar ourselves in and let the rest of the world go hang?' He stood by her, smiling at her, and she remembered thinking last night that the night would probably come when she and Allan would lock the door and be together for ever. Suddenly that seemed less likely. But if it wasn't Allan it certainly wouldn't be Peter with whom she would spend the rest of her life.

'For how long?' she asked.

'Till half past seven in the morning.' She pretended to consider that.

'About eight hours too long,' she said.

The phone rang as they came out of the kitchen, and as Peter answered it she went to the turret window. There was very little activity below. The early church-goers were still in church. The pub wasn't open yet.

That was a business call, because this was the voice in which he had taken the call in Andy's flat: cool, clipped, wasting no words.

Janna turned, almost against her will, and when he put down the phone he smiled at her and came across the room to join her at the window. 'Trouble?' she asked.

'Nothing that won't wait until tomorrow.'

'You sound like another man on the phone.'

'I am.' He looked down as she had been doing, and he would see what she saw, a sleepy Sunday morning in the village. 'I've got a compartmented mind,' he said. A lot of closed doors, nothing getting more than its fair share of room.

Janna felt sorry for the girls who went too hopefully into a relationship with him. The ones who wanted more than a man who was around from time to time. But that was fine by her, she wasn't looking for more than casual friendship, and already the morning was different from her usual run of weekend mornings.

She said, 'I used to like standing at this window.' Peter didn't ask when; he remembered she had said she played up here as a child. 'So do I,' he said, although Janna doubted if he spent much time looking out of windows.

He brought a couple of chairs forward and they sat there, and she told him who lived in all the houses. He had no idea. He knew the landlord of the pub, he'd used that sometimes, but he didn't know his neighbours.

Janna had known most of them all her life. They were her friends and when Peter asked, 'You've always lived here?' she nodded.

'I was born in the cottage.'

'You live there alone now?'

'Since my father died, eight months ago.' Grief could still flood back when she said, 'my father died'. The words still pierced her and she said quickly, 'You live in London most of the time, don't you?'

'I live in hotels most of the time, but I have a flat near my office.'

'Is that like this?'

'Smaller.'

'Did you design this yourself?'

'No. Except for instructions on how I wanted it. You've got a caller.' Down below Allan had crossed the green and was heading up the lane towards Janna's Place.

'He's decided you didn't stay the night,' she said. She watched Allan go round the back, the door was open. It took him a few minutes to find out that the house was empty before he reappeared and headed in this direction. He couldn't see her if he looked up, but she still pushed her chair back a fraction. 'What's he going to do for lunch? He expected to eat with me.'

'That's his problem,' said Peter.

'He'll be coming to see if I'm at Betsy's.' Betsy didn't know where she was, but Allan could come up here after he had seen Betsy.

'Today's mine,' said Peter. 'I'm three hundred miles away tomorrow.' He could have been three hundred miles away today when that phone rang. 'Isn't it?' he said, and the question was a challenge.

'Yes,' she said quietly. If Allan came to the door she would send him away. Not for ever, of course. Knowing Peter would only fill a tiny part of her life, just as she would only occupy a very small compartment in his mind, but she would spend today with him.

Nobody knocked on the door. Allan wouldn't stay long at Betsy's—he wasn't that fond of Betsy and Andy— but he didn't come up here. Janna didn't see him leave because she got up to shoo Punch off the dark green velvet chair.

Peter laughed and said, 'Leave him where he is. He's a dog of discernment.' Because he didn't like Allan or because he had chosen the biggest, softest armchair? She pulled him off all the same and he flopped down in a patch of sunshine.

As well as the modernistic colour-splash painting there was a study of strange green and blue flowers on the wall by the dining table. Janna looked at them both, and when Peter asked, 'Do you like them?' she said, 'They're charming,' which was how he had described her father's work. She wouldn't have hung them on her own walls, but they looked right for this apartment.

She and Peter had different tastes, but—like his home and his pictures—he was different, and exciting. He *was* exciting. He was the only man she'd come across who could make her spine tingle just by passing close to her. Physically and mentally he quickened her responses. When she was talking to him her mind felt livelier.

But some of the antagonism lingered. She might well have a flaming row with him before the day ended. She suspected that he would turn to ice in a flaming row and was surprised at herself, a peace-loving girl, for thinking that it might be interesting to find out.

In the end he operated the microwave oven and they both sat down to a meal of coq au vin, followed by blackcurrant pie. They fed Punch as they ate, against hygiene and training, but once Peter started feeding him that was it. It was a meal Janna would remember. This man's humour and charm were devastatingly attractive and he made her feel prettier and wittier than she had ever been before.

As they drank coffee and ate cheese and biscuits he said, 'What do you suggest for the afternoon's entertainment?' and she suddenly felt that the big bed in the next room was right in this room with them, and her cheeks flushed and her breath quickened. She knew what he was thinking, and if he came and put his arms around her, or just reached across and touched her, she could very well lose her senses for a while.

Her voice sounded squeaky. 'I think I should like to go for a walk. Punch needs to go out.'

'Good old Punch,' said Peter. 'Shall we drive out somewhere?'

'Yes, please.' She was on her feet.

'Don't run,' said Peter. 'Please don't run.'

She wasn't running from him as much as from herself. She had read that phrase lots of times and it was making sense now, because if she stayed here this afternoon, into evening, perhaps into night, she could be the one who turned to look at that bedroom door.

But she made herself smile and say, 'I'm not running,' and sit down again and finish her coffee.

# CHAPTER FOUR

LAST night Janna had sat in that cab bringing them from the hotel, stiff with indignation and as far away as she could from Peter. Now in the car she was completely relaxed, smiling at him when he turned and smiled at her, as they reached the busier main road.

Punch sprawled on the back seat and a couple walking along, taking a Sunday afternoon stroll, recognised Janna and stared until the car was out of sight. Since her father died nobody had seen her in a car with any man but Allan. Peter Craig's Jensen was known, and what was Janna Wyman doing with him? they asked each other.

Janna was far from sure herself. Except that she was driving somewhere and feeling cheerful and irresponsible, as though years had fallen off her shoulders. 'Right or left?' asked Peter.

'Second left,' she said, which took them out into the lanes again and away towards other villages. But she hadn't stopped to think before she spoke. It was too late to go far. Somewhere they could stop the car and walk a while, and talk some more.

He hadn't told her much about himself, and she wanted to know the simple things such as where he was born and if his parents were still alive. Things his colleagues would know. Likes and dislikes, the kind of books he read, the music he listened to.

She wanted to know how it would feel if he stroked her cheek, the touch of his hand on her breast, and at her sharp intake of breath he asked, 'What is it?'

It was as though she had felt him touch her. 'It's warm in here,' she said. 'May I open the window?' and the breeze cooled her hot cheeks, lifting her hair.

'How about that?' said Peter, after they had driven about eight miles and gone through another three villages. He slowed down so that she could read the poster stuck on a wall. 'Open today. Gardens of Yelverstone Grange. Proceeds towards Village Hall Restoration Fund. Entrance 50p. Children & O.A.Ps 10p. Teas.'

'Why ever not?' she said.

'They're rather splendid.'

'You've seen them?'

'Yes.'

'All right. It's the gardens of the Grange.'

Janna had passed the high walls and the iron-scrolled gates before, but she had never gone through the gates. She knew nothing about the house, nor who lived there. Cars were parked in a field nearby and scattered groups were strolling towards the Grange.

Just inside the gates a man and a girl sat at a small wooden table, with a roll of tickets and a biscuit tin containing the takings.

'Two, please,' said Peter, when the family of four ahead of them had been dealt with, and the man rolled off a couple of tickets. The girl had been making an entry in a little notebook, but she looked up when she heard his voice and squealed,

'*Peter!*'

She was very young, seventeen at the most, with babyfine hair cut in a pretty little flipped-up cap. Her blue eyes opened wide in delight and her cheeks pinked. 'Oh, Peter!' she said again.

'How are you?' he smiled.

'All right. You're all right, of course.' She looked at Janna as Peter moved on, there was a small queue waiting. 'See you later?' the girl called after them.

'Yes, of course,' he said. Whoever she was she had a crush on him, and as soon as they were out of her hearing Janna said crisply,

'Isn't she rather young for you?'

'Much too young.' He smiled at her. 'How old are you?'

'Twenty-one.'

'I'm thirty-four, did you know that?'

They were passing a half-timbered barn, with a dove-cote in the roof. Plump white birds sat around on the eaves and fluttered overhead. Janna watched the flight of one and said, 'I cooked your birthday party.'

'You're very young.' She looked younger than she was, without much make-up left, and her hair windblown; and compared to him she was very inexperienced. Compared to almost anybody she was very inexperienced. She wouldn't be surprised if that seventeen-year-old was more experienced, she thought dourly, and realised that for the first time in her life she was feeling jealous.

It was an unpleasant sensation. If she was getting an attack of this every time a woman lit up, seeing him, this had better be their last outing together. She said wryly, 'Most of the time I don't feel so young.'

'Neither do I.' His face was boyish, he moved like an athlete, but his brown hair had a touch of grey here and there, and there was always the thoughtfulness in the eyes. 'Except with you,' he said.

It was an obvious line, he probably didn't mean it at all, but she was going to believe he did because she felt young when she was with him.

She had had responsibilities ever since her mother died. She had taken over the running of the house then although she was still a schoolgirl. Her father was wonderful, but he was a man who had never been expected to do a hand's turn after his day's work, except paint his pictures.

All her life Janna had cared for anything that needed care. Her present 'menagerie' was a continuation of a long line of birds and beasts that nobody wanted. She liked being needed. She didn't regret the years she had encouraged and looked after her father, and Allan had the same needs, but she did feel younger and more alive with Peter.

Even that pang of jealousy was part of this heightened awareness, and walking through rock gardens, stopping to peer into a little lake where coloured fish flashed just beneath the dark surface, everything seemed brighter and sharper and clearer

The gardens were splendid, just as he had said, and the house was Jacobean, mellow red brick and tall twisted chimneys and mullioned windows. There were 'follies' around—a wide avenue of beech trees that led nowhere, except to a bank that dropped down into a field, but that looked imposing and beautiful from the great lawn; and a round summer house like a small temple, lined with Delft tiles, and with a marble seat around the wall.

The summer house overlooked a wide sweep of the gardens, and as Janna sat, looking through the open circle of the window and breathing deep in rapture, she felt Peter's hand on her hair and looked up into his face. 'Is this what you want?' he asked.

'Good heavens, *no*!' She would be as likely to covet Buckingham Palace. Houses like this were for looking at and wondering at, and going home and talking about. Although it was lived in, possibly by the girl at the gate. She had the air of wealth about her, less flamboyantly than Caroline, but it was there.

Peter hadn't told her who the girl was, nor if they were going to see her afterwards, and she wouldn't ask. She was much too young, he had said, but the memory of that delighted face and squeal of recognition threw a small shadow on the day.

She asked, 'How about you? Is it your ambition to own a house like this?'

'It's a millstone.' Two children began to run up the steps leading to the summer arbour, squabbling about who would get there first ... 'Beat you to the top,' and a woman's voice rose fretfully, 'Diane, will you *stop* that!'

'If I'd wanted a stately home I'd have had one by now,' said Peter.

He wasn't boasting. It was a fact. But all that money from people in trouble, it didn't seem right.

There was a howl from outside and a small girl shot into the arbour with a broad grin on her face. The howling went on and the woman's voice snapped, 'Oh, do get up, Clyde!'

Clyde was picking himself up as Janna and Peter walked down the steps. His mother gave them a weary grin and sighed, 'Kids!' and Janna smiled back.

'I reckon Diane booted her brother off the top,' said Peter.

'She could make a good lawyer,' said Janna.

'Or a good thug.'

'In which case she'll need a good lawyer. You can't lose, can you?'

'I hope not.' He took her hand, lacing his fingers with hers, and she wondered what he was thinking about. If he was thinking of her it was as well he didn't know that she couldn't have dragged her hand away to save her life.

'TEAS,' said the notice, with a black arrow pointing towards a small courtyard. 'I could use a cup of tea,' said Janna. 'Could you bear to push a tray round?'

As they took a tray up to the extemporised counter—composed of boards on trestles, covered with bright red shiny paper—she said, 'I don't suppose you do this often.'

'Not often,' he agreed.

The choice was straightforward: tea or soft drinks, rock cakes or scones. 'I'll stay with tea,' said Peter, and Janna took a cake for herself. There were little tables around, mostly full of sightseers who had walked them-selves weary. It was late afternoon by now, the shadows were long and the sun had dipped almost to the horizon.

They found two chairs in a corner, and put their tray on the ground, and drank some of the rather weak tea, Janna nibbled on her rather hard rock cake. They talked and laughed, and she felt as though they had been inseparable for years.

And yet she knew no more about him than she had known yesterday. He didn't talk about himself, perhaps that was why everything was so companionable. Long-time friends didn't tell you their life stories, they just talked about what was going on now.

She knew there were things that she disliked about him. Peter the lawyer in action, as Andy had said she should see him, would be anathema to her; but this Peter was a marvellous man. I'll settle for this one, she thought, and hope I never come across his alter-ego. She was no Pandora, she didn't want to open any doors in the mind and let loose the secrets.

She said, 'You were crafty, not having one of these rock cakes. I think they used cement in the mix.'

'Peter, m'boy!' bellowed a large red-faced man, who was standing in the middle of the little courtyard. 'Been looking everywhere for you.' He marched towards them in a dead straight line, without sparing a glance for what might be in his way, and by sheer luck not knocking down anyone or anything. 'Splendid to see you,' he said, pumping Peter's arm. 'Dotty told us you were here.'

He had a voice that carried, even now he was under the impression that he was conducting a private conversation. 'You're not eating that tack?' he exclaimed in such horror that Janna almost dropped her rock cake, and so did half the others who had bought cakes. The ladies serving teas exchanged exasperated glances and Janna and Peter exchanged amused ones.

'Come inside,' said the booming man, and led them through the nearest door. 'Flaming bunfight,' he muttered, striding off down a passage. 'Maudie and her old women!'

Janna presumed she would be told who he was in time. He had to be the owner of the place, nobody else would get away with this; and when he marched into a very beautiful drawing room, that couldn't have changed much since Georgian days, the woman who got up smiling was probably Maudie.

Maudie could have been in her fifties. She wore a camel cashmere skirt and jumper, and a camel and blue silk scarf. She had a handsome face, a little gaunt, and smooth brown hair taken neatly back; and she was as pleased to see Peter as the booming man and the girl at the gate. Although the girl at the gate had looked as though she would have liked to throw her arms around him.

Maudie was the lady of the house, and her husband was George Adams. They both shook hands with Janna, and another tea was brought in, a much more elegant affair than the one outside, with thin cut sandwiches and cakes that melted in the mouth. Peter, it seemed, was a friend of the family who hadn't been near them for ages.

He pleaded work and they believed him. George Adams talked to Peter about some building that was going up on some land he owned, and Maudie asked Janna where she came from and who her parents were. She looked blank when Janna said that her father had taught at a comprehensive school, and murmured something about the stock market. She was obviously thinking of Caroline. Then she gave Janna a dazzling smile and said it was sweet of them to come and see the gardens, and the village hall was such a good cause and the trouble was rising damp.

What Janna would have liked to do was wander round, get up and examine the paintings, touch the marble fireplace and look closer at the detail in the pair of famille rose porcelain vases on the mantelshelf. But sitting here, having tea, was quite an event.

They were half way through tea when the girl from

the gate came rushing in and right across to Peter with outstretched hands.

He got up, took her hands and held her at arms' length as though he wanted to see her better. They made an attractive picture, the tall smiling man and the tall smiling girl. She was leggier than she had appeared, sitting taking tickets at the gate. In white flared jeans her legs seemed to go on for ever, making Janna feel dumpy and dowdy.

'Why didn't you tell us you were coming?' she demanded.

'We didn't know. We saw the poster.' He included Janna. 'This is Dorothea,' he said. 'And this is Janna.'

Janna began to say, 'How do you do,' but Dorothea tossed her an offhand 'Hi!' and went on smiling at Peter. 'Now you are here you'll stay, won't you, you'll stay the night?'

She was older than sixteen or seventeen, Janna decided. More likely eighteen or nineteen, and she was propositioning Peter right in front of them all, whether her parents realised it or not. As for Janna, she might have been in another room. Dorothea had hardly looked at her, and she suddenly felt very angry.

She said, 'That's kind of you, but we both have to be at work early in the morning,' and was astonished at her presumption in answering for him. It was bad enough answering for herself, because Dorothea wasn't asking her.

Dorothea was astonished too. She gasped and Peter said, 'That's right,' and Maud said it was a pity, and would they come another time, any time.

They stayed for about an hour, during which Dorothea spent most of the time sitting on the arm of Peter's chair, and Maud went out occasionally to check on her team of helpers, or perhaps to help. There were no more sightseers coming in now.

George Adams went on about the cost of living and

upkeep of a place like this, and Dorothea pulled faces and said that she was into a modelling career. A friend of a friend had arranged a TV commercial for her, and had they seen her drinking a glass of pink sparkling stuff? 'No,' said Peter, 'but we'll certainly look out for it.'

When they left the takings were being added up on a table in the hall and the main gates were closed. They were the last out, unless there was anyone still wandering around the gardens in the gloaming, who hadn't heard the 'We are closing now, thank you for coming' through a loudspeaker.

When Janna heard it, floating through the windows, she had thought that if they'd used George Adams they wouldn't have needed an amplifier, and Peter had smiled at her at that moment as though he'd read her thoughts.

'Altogether,' said Janna, as they got Punch back into the car—he had slept all the time they were away but was ready for a quick dash to the nearest tree—'that was well worth the fifty pence. I did enjoy my tea.'

'Did you enjoy the Adams?'

'Oh yes. And the house. It's an incredible house.' They drove out of the field, past the long wall. 'Have you known them long?' she asked.

'The old man's a friend of my father's.' He didn't tell her anything about his father, and she couldn't tell anything from his voice. As he'd used the present tense his father must still be living.

'They seemed very pleased to see you,' she said.

A slight smile touched his lips. 'George once signed some papers he shouldn't have touched with a bargepole and nearly landed in the dock. I got him out of it.'

'He seems a bit eccentric.' And stubborn. Not the sort to take advice until he was forced to listen.

'He's an old fool,' said Peter, with more impatience than affection.

'And you don't have much time for fools?'

'I suffer them,' he said briefly.

'At a price?'

'It was cheap at the price. He and his family could have ended up skint.'

If Peter had saved her father from what might have been a criminal charge that could partly account for Dorothea's attitude. But not in the name of friendship; he had charged, it seemed, the rate for the job. And if he had been overweight and six inches shorter Dorothea would not, Janna knew, have invited him to stay the night. Nor said, 'Now you will phone, won't you?' when they left.

She asked, 'Shall you be going back?' and when he said,

'Not if I can help it,' she felt ridiculously pleased.

On the way home they drew in off the road at the highest point in the hills, and got out of the car, taking deep breaths of the fragrant night air. Punch rambled around and Janna stood with Peter's arm around her, waiting for him to kiss her.

It was lovely, this waiting moment. It felt like standing on a high diving board must feel to an expert diver, the breathless moment before they lose contact with firmness beneath their feet and become part of the rushing elements.

She lifted her face, her lips parted slightly in instinctive invitation, and his arm tightened around her shoulders, but instead of kissing her he said, 'What do you want from life?'

'What?' She hadn't expected him to speak just then, she was bewildered and disappointed.

'You don't want a house like the Grange,' he said. 'What do you want?'

It hadn't seemed the time nor the place for words, but she said, 'I want my business to succeed. In a small way —not take off, not make a fortune. I want a peaceful life.'

She supposed that was what she wanted. But then

Peter kissed her and every thought in her mind dissolved. She wanted the kissing to go on. She wanted to forget everything and let go and let herself sink down into the depths. But she didn't want the guilt she might feel in the morning if that happened, and she drew back the tiniest fraction and the kissing stopped.

'A peaceful life,' said Peter. He brushed her hair from her face very gently. 'Unlikely,' he said. 'I see a period of unrest ahead.'

She could see it too, and feel it in every nerve, and a period of unrest might be exhilarating so long as she remembered that it couldn't last, because he didn't have that much time to spare.

He was an expert kisser, he would make love with a devastating expertise, but she must remember that this was likely to be a short-term relationship. She smiled and said, 'When you're this way again look me up.'

'It should be Thursday.'

That would give her three whole days for carrying on her business and her life in the steady old way, and then on Thursday she would see Peter. She said, 'I may have Thursday free. Again I may not, but you can always ask, can't you?'

'I'll do that.' He must know she was unlikely to be booked up, except by Allan. She should be getting conscience pangs about Allan, but Allan didn't own her, and with Peter so near she found it hard to think clearly about any other man.

She called to Punch, who was snuffling along the grass verge, and said, 'I should be getting home.'

'Of course,' said Peter. 'You've got the menagerie waiting.'

He opened the car door for her, and turned on the radio, and when they reached her home and she said, 'Thursday then; unless I find I can't make it or you get delayed at the office, or at court or wherever,' he said, 'There's always that risk.'

He didn't suggest coming in. He didn't kiss her again. He drove to the top of the cul-de-sac that was her lane, and raised a hand and smiled as he passed her, still standing on the pavement.

Janna had come back and locked up before she left, and now she let herself in by the front door. She had enjoyed every minute of her day and she hurried through her chores, putting Freddy into his shed. Then she locked up and ran a bath, feeding Punch and Judy while it was filling.

After her bath she was going straight to bed, because then if Allan came, wanting to know where she had been, she would have every excuse for not answering the door.

The bathroom was full of steam when she went in. She turned off the hot tap and ran a trickle of cold water, she was in no hurry. She poured in a little bath essence and watched the water turn green and foaming, and sniffed the rising aroma of herbs.

She undressed slowly and slid down into the water, letting the grime of the day melt away. She sometimes solved problems lying in the bath, there was something very soothing about the slow swirl of the water around her limbs. Not that she had any problems tonight. She had another friend, another man in her life, but no problems, because she would be very wary about any emotional dealings with Peter Craig.

She soaked and drifted, in the caressing lapping of the scented water, until the water grew cooler, and she stretched to turn on the hot tap with her toes—a trick she had learned as a child. She must have pushed harder than she meant because the next thing she knew the water was gushing and scalding, so that she leapt up and back with a strangled shriek. Then she hurriedly turned off the tap and scrambled out of the bath.

She wasn't scalded, but the whole silly thing had

shaken her, because until then she had felt so safe and comfortable.

She went upstairs, Punch padding up behind her, and got into bed. Punch settled down on the rug at the foot of the bed and was snuffling and snoring almost at once. There were those who would say she was heading for trouble going around with Peter Craig, who would tell her she was bound to get her heart scalded. But you couldn't get burned by a cold man, and that was Peter Craig. Under the charm he was cold.

She said 'I don't like him, just his company, so that's all right, isn't it? I'm not risking anything.'

Her answer was a soft snore from Punch. It usually was when she talked to him at night.

The fine weather had broken next morning. There was a nip in the air, perceptible as soon as she surfaced from under the bedclothes, and the sky was heavy. It had been warm for several weeks, but now the hoped-for hot summer seemed in the balance, and she put on a warmer dress than the one she had planned to wear.

The cottage was mostly heated by paraffin heaters, she hadn't needed to bother with them lately. An immersion heater kept the water hot, and last thing at night she sometimes put on a bar of the electric fire. But this morning she lit the heater in the shop before she sat down to breakfast. Customers weren't going to strip and try on if they got goose pimples.

She was eating cornflakes when Allan arrived. 'Where were you yesterday?' he asked as soon as she opened the kitchen door, and she told him,

'I went out with Peter.'

He had got no information from Betsy or Andrew, but he was sure they were keeping something from him, and he had almost gone up to Peter Craig's apartment. Pride had stopped him, and the fact that Craig made him feel

like a loser. He didn't fancy a confrontation with Peter
Craig, but he told himself it was only pride that had
prevented him climbing those stairs yesterday morning
and knocking on the top floor door.

This morning, before he left for school, he was ready
to hear Janna's explanation. She had answered his
question readily enough, but having answered she just
sat down again, looking bright and luminous, as though
the sun was still shining instead of being hidden under a
blanket of sullen grey clouds.

He said, 'We were supposed to be going out,' and she
had forgotten that. She said,

'Oh, sorry,' and smiled, and he found her cheerfulness
irritating. He had only a few minutes before he had to
be driving himself to work, he didn't want to argue with
her, but when he asked,

'Did you have a good time then?' it sounded waspish.

'Yes,' she said simply.

'Of course you're entitled to your friends.' Punch, who
had been out in the garden, had followed him into the
house and was standing on guard, eyes fixed on him.
'But I thought we were enough for each other,' said
Allan plaintively. He didn't make many friends. 'I've
never looked at another girl since I met you.'

Yesterday had been the first change for Janna too, and
she heard herself say gently, 'Perhaps you should,' and
was sorry at the hurt look on Allan's face. But she
couldn't promise not to see Peter again. She said, 'You're
going to be late. I'll cook an apple pie for tonight.'

Comfort me with apples . . . where had she heard
that? What she meant was—things haven't really
changed. I know you're kinder and more caring than
Peter, but I just need a break. I don't like him like I
like you, but he makes me laugh and it won't last long.

'I'll see you tonight.' Allan looked hard at her with his
beautiful grey eyes, and she said,

'Yes, of course,' and as he went out Punch growled and

Allan gave him a look of frustrated dislike as though he wanted to kick him.

'That wasn't called for, Punch,' said Janna, when the door closed. 'You've got no tact, have you?'

Betsy got over as soon as she could, and her opening remark was the same as Allan's. 'Where were you?'

'Out with Peter,' Janna said again.

She was in the shop now, she had been open for about five minutes, opening at nine although customers rarely turned up much before ten. Living on the premises it was as easy to come in here, right after breakfast, and tidy up stock or deal with the mail.

This morning Janna was choosing a suit and a dress for herself. Her off duty wardrobe was small, but if she was going around with Peter she didn't want to look less than her best. She suspected that it was seeing her dressed for the evening out that had made him realise she was attractive. So he fancied her, and if it was only a surface attraction—well, that was how she felt about him too.

'So what happened?' asked Betsy.

'We had lunch in his apartment,' said Janna, 'and then we went out. He'll be back on Thursday and that's more or less a date.'

Betsy veered between triumph and trepidation. It was great that Peter Craig was attracted to Janna, but she didn't want Janna made miserable when the affair ended. Because right now Janna looked—perhaps the word was 'radiant'. Shining. Eyes bright, skin glowing, even her hair seemed to crackle with life as she went along the row of dresses, swishing the hangers apart.

'Did he—?' Betsy gulped. 'Did you—?' If they had been up in that apartment alone all day, Peter was very much a man of the world, and after eight months of Allan—who was a right drip in Betsy's opinion—it seemed more than likely that they had. Which could account for Janna's smile. But Janna laughed and said,

'Just a goodnight kiss—and that was out in the open. Don't worry, I'm not falling in love with him.' She took a dress and held it in front of her, looking at her reflection in the long mirror. She said, 'I still don't really like him, but I've never met anyone like him before.' She wasn't looking at the dress any longer, although she still held it at her shoulders as she talked to Betsy's reflection.

'He's a machine, the way he can shut off parts of his mind. No wonder his girl-friends get tetchy! But he's sexy and amusing and highly intelligent, and six months of Peter Craig around from time to time should ginger life up.

'If I found I was getting too fond of him then I'd run, I promise you, because I don't think there'll ever be a permanent place for any girl in his life, and if he tried to make one it wouldn't be for a girl like me. He'd pick an asset to his career, heaven help her.'

Betsy nodded, and Janna went on, 'But I am enjoying myself, and if he doesn't ring on Thursday he will ring again quite soon, and I shall dress myself up and go out with him again. And why not?'

She looked at herself as she asked that, and then at Betsy, and Betsy said, 'Why not? So long as you know it's not going to last.'

Janna had no doubts there, and they spent the next quarter of an hour choosing a dress she could wear on Thursday, if Peter Craig was back from representing clients who were raising several million pounds to finance an oilfield.

Allan came right round after work, as soon as he had parked his car. He came into the shop carrying a box of Turkish Delight and Janna, who had a customer in, turning round and round in front of the mirror wondering whether to buy a skirt, said, 'Be with you in a minute.'

Allan could have gone through into the cottage, but Punch usually lay on the other side of the connecting door. So he went back into the street again; and waited until the customer left.

Then he handed over the Turkish Delight and gave Janna a kiss to go with it. She was touched, the kiss meant he wasn't wanting a break and neither did she. And the Turkish Delight brought a lump to her throat, because it was what her father sometimes brought her. He used to eat most of it, it was his favourite sweetmeat and Allan knew that, and it was a very nice gesture.

Allan was being nice. They had supper in Janna's house—she had made the apple pie, and she whipped up a spaghetti dish while Allan read the morning paper.

He did ask, 'Are you seeing Craig again?' and when she said,

'I expect so,' he sighed and said,

'That's up to you, of course. I can't dictate what you do twenty-four hours of the day.'

He was being very dignified, very reasonable. He wasn't suggesting they married or became engaged because, at the moment, he didn't feel like the responsibility of a wife. But Janna was an exceptional girl, and during the day he had reasoned that Craig wasn't going to take her away permanently. He would have preferred it if she had never met the man, but she had, and there was going to be a brief affair. But she didn't want to finish their friendship, which meant she would still cook for Allan and care about him, and in the end come back to him and think herself lucky he was still waiting.

He was not going to create any scenes. He was going to carry on as nearly as possible as they were at present. 'Are you seriously interested in Craig?' he asked her, and was reassured when she said,

'Not seriously, no,' because she didn't have to stop and consider, and her answer, he was sure, was sincere.

They passed the kind of evening that had occurred regularly in the past eight months. Allan had brought over what he had written over the weekend and Janna typed it. She was self-taught with two fingers, but she rattled along quite briskly and Allan couldn't type at all. He had been paying for his typing to be done, before he discovered that Janna had bought a typewriter for business letters.

When she'd finished they settled down to watch a late movie on television, and she hoped that Allan wouldn't try to make love to her because it was the last thing she wanted. She liked having him here, everything about him was familiar and reassuring, but she didn't want him to kiss her or touch her. If she responded it would be kindness, not desire, because tonight she was restless with an alien fire.

Something was burning her up. Sitting quietly beside Allan was an effort, and only a third of the way through the film she said, 'Would you be mortally offended if I said goodnight? I can't keep my eyes open.'

'Did you have a strenuous time yesterday?'

He expected her to flare at that, but she said, 'Not particularly,' as though she missed his meaning.

'You want me to go?' he said.

'Yes, please.'

So he went, and it was a lie that she was tired. She wasn't. She was restless and Allan was getting on her nerves, so that when she shut the door on him she almost danced around the living room from sheer relief.

She could have danced all night if there had been someone to dance with. As it was she could only get ready for bed, and take a book up with her to try and read herself to sleep.

When the phone went it was past midnight, and her heart jumped because it was so late. She couldn't imagine who could be calling this late and she turned on all the lights as she came downstairs. Calls after midnight were rare enough to be scarey. She wasn't giving her number, and if it was a man's voice that she didn't recognise she was putting that phone right down.

She recognised Peter as soon as he spoke, but because it hadn't occurred to her that he might be calling she needed a moment to get herself together before she could speak normally. 'Hello?' he said. 'Janna?'

'Yes, I'm still here.' She laughed softly. 'This is a late call. I thought you might be a heavy breather.'

'Do you get many?'

'Now you mention it, no, but neither do I have many friends who call after midnight.'

'I'm sorry, did I disturb you?'

'Oh *no*.' She didn't want him to think that, she was very glad he had phoned her. 'It's all right, you can go back to bed,' she said when Punch came yawning into the room.

'I did disturb you,' said Peter, and she was fogged momentarily, then she yelped,

'I was talking to the *dog*!' and he chuckled.

'Do apologise to him for me.'

'He says he doesn't mind.'

They talked for a little while about nothing much. He said that he still hoped to be back on Thursday and he would collect her around eight in the evening. 'Sleep well,' he said. 'Goodnight.'

Janna echoed, 'Goodnight.' When she got back to bed she closed the book, lying open on the counterpane, and turned off the light. She wondered if affairs always started this way, with a fair amount of attention at first, tapering off after a few months.

That had been a pretty prompt phone call. She wondered if she would get another before Thursday, and she curled up, relaxed and suddenly drowsy, falling asleep at once, almost as though she had been waiting for him to say goodnight.

# CHAPTER FIVE

PETER didn't phone again, so Janna had no idea what Thursday evening's plans were, no real certainty that he was coming. But when she took Allan's meal over she mentioned that she was probably going out later.

'With Craig?' Allan hadn't spoken of Peter again since Monday night, but now he looked up suspiciously from the two lamb chops with salad that she had set out for him on the table.

'If he can get away,' she said.

'Get away from where?' and he pushed his plate aside as though his appetite had gone.

'Work,' she said.

'You'll be waiting for him if he does?' He disliked the idea of Janna waiting for Peter Craig. He wanted her to be waiting for him, as she had been for the last eight months.

She shrugged, 'I'll be here. I told him I'd be here.' And Allan told himself that Craig might well not turn up, and if he did Janna was hardly his type. They had nothing to build a relationship on, except that awareness of each other Allan had seen on Sunday morning, and that would fade. Janna might be infatuated, but Peter Craig was hard as nails as well as ten years older. Of course he would tire of her.

'You're being a fool to yourself,' said Allan.

'Could be.' But she smiled as she said it, because she had no intention of being hurt. She didn't much care either way, whether Peter turned up or not. It would be fun if he did, but as she had heard no more she hardly expected him.

All the same she was dressed for going out, in the pink

silk dress she had worn all day, and although she had cooked for Allan she herself ate hardly anything. She made a cup of tea and opened a pack of Garibaldi biscuits. Then she started on the typing she would do tonight if Peter didn't come.

It was Allan's book, and she knew the characters by now as well as she knew her neighbours in the village. Although the setting was a hotel in the Highlands of Scotland, where they were all snowed in.

There were eight main characters, and they had problems that they spent a lot of time discussing, with flashbacks on their lives. It was a very clever book, complicated but clever.

One woman had been rhapsodising for two pages, because the snow reminded her of a day in Switzerland five years before. It must have been very beautiful in Switzerland, but suddenly Janna caught herself in the middle of a gusty sigh and heard herself mutter, 'They do go *on*!'

Of course she wasn't bored, it was a lyrical descriptive passage, but she turned over the next few handwritten pages and found that Marguerite was still looking up at the mountains and nothing was happening.

Nothing was happening here either. It was half eight now, with no sign of Peter, and the typewriter ribbon needed changing, and she'd be taking a chance doing that in her shell pink outfit.

He wasn't coming, and she might as well get into jeans and make herself comfortable. Then she'd take Punch for a walk to the end of the village. They'd call on friends and spend the evening there.

She wasn't disappointed. It had only been a 'maybe' date and it didn't matter. She came out of the bathroom singing, but the knock on the front door choked off her song as though a hand had been clapped across her mouth.

It could be anybody at all. Most friends walked in

through the back door, but some knocked at the front door and it could be anybody. She went quite slowly to open it, Punch at her heels, but when she saw Peter standing there she was unprepared for the rush of happiness that took her breath and then made her laugh aloud.

He smiled at her, almost laughing too. 'I thought you might be out,' he said. 'I've tried to get you twice since six o'clock. I didn't know until the last minute that I could make it.'

'I've been out.' So she had. 'Across the way and walking round the paddock. Do come in.'

As he stepped in he reached for her, and drew her towards him and kissed her, and she felt the kiss all through her body. Then he said, 'Hello.'

'Hello. Are you expecting me to feed you?'

He shook his head. 'Can you give me half an hour and then we'll go out and eat?'

'I'd better change myself,' she said, as though she had been dressed like this all evening, and hadn't sat waiting for him until ten minutes ago.

He noticed Punch, as he released her and Punch wagged his tail. 'Hello, feller,' said Peter, and patted him. 'Are you sleeping well?'

'No more late night calls,' she said. 'Half an hour, then.'

It was seeing him that did it, having him touch her. The last day or two she had almost put him out of her mind, but when she was close to him the power he could have over her struck her forcibly. Perhaps it was time she took a risk or two. Life had always been safe for her. Starting up her business with a small bank loan had been the chanciest thing she'd ever done.

They ate at a restaurant, recently opened and specialising in German food, with a decor that was supposed to look like a classy beer cellar. There were customers waiting when they arrived, sipping drinks at the bar, but they were seated immediately, by a waiter who looked surprised to find himself in a costume that included leather shorts. He had very thin white legs and knobbly knees, and Janna felt someone should have told him that a touch of instant tan might have helped.

The other tables were filled. Peter hadn't known he could make it until the last minute, but this table had been booked in his name so that no time was wasted when they arrived. She couldn't imagine him hanging around, wasting time and energy. They had wandered round that garden at Yelverstone Grange, but not aimlessly even there. He always seemed to know where he was going.

The food was delicious, and she set out to amuse, to sing for her supper, because there would be no other payment. They would end tonight in separate beds, although he might have other plans, making smiling love to her across the table as they ate.

Once their eyes met and the gaze held so long that Janna became dizzy. She jerked her head to break the little spell, as though he was physically holding her. And when he leaned towards her, touching her hand, talking so that no one else could hear, it was all part of the closeness and very pleasurable.

She surrendered to the delight of the evening, and told him about her last three days, embroidering on what had been pretty uneventful. She wasn't exactly inventing, just making her customers larger than life.

Peter didn't tell her anything about what he'd been doing, he kept business and pleasure apart, but Allan had never concentrated on her like this nor made her feel half so attractive.

'Was that Allan's book by the typewriter?' Peter asked her. She said yes, it was, and told him a little about it, and he said that the characters sounded like some of his clients and had they thought of consulting a good lawyer.

'It isn't funny,' she said. She wondered for a moment if she could have given the impression that Allan was writing a comedy, but Peter said,

'I'll bet it isn't,' and she found herself defending Allan's masterpiece.

'It's very touching, very moving.' It *was*, and she went on hotly because he looked unconvinced and he had no right to belittle when he couldn't possibly know, 'It's *life*. Do you think life's funny?'

'Sometimes it has to be,' he said quietly, 'or all the thinking people would go mad,' and she glimpsed a bleakness in his eyes that seemed darker than the troubles of Allan's characters.

She asked, 'Has it been that kind of week?' and he said,

'It usually is.' Then he took another sip of wine and asked her how long Allan had been writing the book, and talked about writers he knew—whose names she knew— and it was all lighthearted again.

They drove home through a drizzling night; there was no getting out of the car tonight, no moon and stars to look up at, and Janna wondered if Peter would drive to the Old Vicarage, taking it for granted she would go up to his apartment. Or to her home and expect her to ask him in.

She was determined, but it wasn't going to be easy, because although she had had experience at smiling and saying no she had never had dealings with a man as experienced as Peter Craig. Nor with one she found any- where near as attractive.

She would have loved to finish the evening in his arms, but she wouldn't, because so far as she was concerned that would have changed everything. She would be emotionally involved after that, and she would suffer for it. So no, thank you; but as they got nearer to the village she could feel a pulse fluttering in her throat and the palms of her hands were turning clammy. She was going to make a mess of this. She wasn't going to be able to put it so that it didn't sound awkward and naïve. Or scared stupid.

If he took her straight home she could scramble out of the car and start saying goodnight, and what a lovely evening she had had. He'd surely take the hint. If she could get her keys out of her purse now she could have the door open in a few seconds. But what if he followed her in? He'd hardly use force, he wouldn't need to use force. Another few seconds in the darkness, with his mouth on her mouth and his hands caressing her, and she might not be able to tell him to go.

Just outside the village he drew off the road, on to the grass verge, and turned to her with the car engine idling. He wouldn't be intending to make love to her with the engine ticking over. Even for the briefest of goodnight kisses he would have turned off the ignition.

He said, 'Will you come back with me?' and she closed her eyes because she needed to shut out his face or she might have said yes. But she could still feel him close to her, and she ached to say, 'Yes.' Or to say nothing, just put her lips against his skin and creep closer and let him hold her tighter and tighter.

She said, 'Don't you have to be leaving early in the morning?'

'Very early.' She opened her eyes and he was looking at her, and he might have been smiling. 'But I don't need much sleep.'

'I can believe that.' If he touched her she would start stammering, but he didn't, and she said, 'But it's still goodnight. I hope you don't mind.'

She was pleased that her voice sounded light and steady, and he said, 'Of course I mind,' with just the right rueful note, and she knew that the danger was over because he didn't mind that much.

If he had done he would have exerted a little more pressure. He hadn't even said, 'Please come,' or told her how much he wanted her. They both knew that by asking her to go back he was asking her to sleep with him, but he had accepted her refusal so readily that it could have been a relief to him.

He'd know she expected him to make a token pass, but he was leaving early in the morning, he had had a busy week and it wasn't over. He was probably ready to call it a day.

Of course she was glad, in spite of a niggling feeling that he could have turned off the ignition when they'd stopped, and been a little less brisk about driving away.

But they had established that she was not easily available, and she might as well spell that out again so that there would be no future misunderstandings. She said, 'Lovemaking doesn't mean much to you, does it? But it does to me. I pay my way, but not that way.'

'You more than pay your way, by being here.' He wasn't offended, his voice was smiling. They came down the village street and turned at her lane and as the car drew up he said, 'A platonic affair could make a refreshing change.'

'A change anyway,' she said.

'Yes.' He sounded amused. 'May I ring you?'

'Of course.'

Peter reached across to open her door and got out of the car himself, standing by her as she put her key in the lock. 'I would have been ringing even if you'd said no,' he said. He took her hand, kissing first the knuckles then the palm. 'Don't go away,' he said.

'I won't,' she said. Punch had his nose through the narrow opening of the door, and she went into the house. She had left a light on in the living room and the curtains drawn. This was her own little house where she was always safe and warm, and Punch was waiting with wagging tail and whines of welcome.

She heard the low hum of the car engine passing, to sweep round to the garages behind the Old Vicarage, wondered why he had asked her not to go away. She was a fixture here, he was the one who was always leaving . . .

Janna decided that night that she knew exactly where she stood with Peter. She belonged here. When he stayed at his apartment at the Old Vicarage, and if he had an evening or any part of a weekend free, he would probably contact her and collect her. But while he was away she would be well down the list.

So she wouldn't think about him too much. But she couldn't help asking Betsy questions, and next morning Betsy was filling in Peter Craig's background for Janna. His father was all the family he had—as Janna's father had been—his mother had been dead a long time, but his father was landed gentry up North, and Peter had been born with a silver spoon in his mouth. Public school, university, then into a good law firm and making his name from the start.

'He's been lucky,' said Janna. 'He's never been up against it.' She didn't exactly mean that, when his life's work was doing battle, but it was the kind of background to give you confidence and self-assurance.

'You are interested in him, aren't you?' said Betsy, and Janna replied blithely,

'Interested, but never involved.'

During the next month Peter phoned her once or twice a week, and was down here for a night or two most weeks. When he came down he came for her, and she took time and trouble on her appearance, and it made a welcome break.

Several times she met friends of his. She went to two dinner parties and an evening get-together of the county folk, where one of her customers greeted her as though they were sharing a guilty secret. 'What's up with Marion?' Peter enquired, when that lady passed by with a puckered face, and Janna whispered solemnly,

'She brings the clothes she doesn't want to my shop, and I don't think she's telling anybody.'

He grinned. 'I won't breathe a word,' he promised.

The warm spring weather was turning into a wet summer with brief bright days, and the bright days often seemed to be the ones when she saw Peter. Everyone thought they were having an affair. Allan did; Betsy did. Betsy thought it was Janna's business, she was old enough to know her own mind and Peter was a very attractive man and Betsy wasn't blaming her in any way. Allan didn't talk about it at all.

Allan was in a predicament. Unless he asked Janna to marry him he could hardly complain when she went dashing off with Peter Craig, but he had never seen himself as a married man. It took some thinking about, and in the meantime she was still cooking and typing and encouraging him in his work, they were still very good friends. He was trying to ignore her affair with Craig, confident that it would end one day, and he prided himself on being a broadminded modern bloke. He would have been pleased and very surprised to know that the relationship was platonic.

Janna wondered sometimes whether Peter saw her as an escort service. When she was beautifully dressed, and when she spent time on her hair and her face, she could look as good as any girl around. He could take her anywhere, she thought wryly, and be fairly sure she wasn't going to turn possessive; and—as he had explained before he took her anywhere—that was what he wanted. But she enjoyed herself wherever he took her. Whenever he was with her his masculine vitality always made him a stimulating companion, and the situation could have become sexual if she had shown, ever so slightly, that she was willing.

But she wasn't. Well, not at first, because he *was* cold and calculating. Often Andy lost sleep over cases. Betsy would say, 'Andy was up at three o'clock this morning brewing tea.' He worried about the clients, identified with some of them, but when Janna asked Peter if he felt sorry for the men and women who brought their troubles and their tragedies to him he said, 'It isn't sympathy they're needing. I could bleed for them and it wouldn't help.'

He was right, but it chilled her. Allan seemed to care more about his make-believe characters than Peter did for his real-life clients. Allan would talk passionately for hours about the people in his book, but Peter never talked about his clients. It would have been unprofessional, of course, but Janna felt they were all filed away in those other compartments in his mind, all numbered as points of law.

She was glad that Peter was her companion and not her lover. She saw how people reacted to him, liking him, respecting him, and watched his charm and the stunning brilliance of his mind working on them, and felt that no one was really reaching him.

And yet the spell worked for her too. She looked forward to being with him, and all the time she was with him she knew that he could dissolve her defences if he tried a fraction harder.

He complimented her. 'You look marvellous,' he would tell her. 'You're worth travelling a hundred miles for, any night.' Although she knew he never came down here just to see her. He took her to romantic places, dinners for two as well as other people's houses, and the mood between them was often lightly romantic.

But so was the lovemaking. He could have set her on fire, but he didn't. She thought she was the one who drew back from the goodnight kiss, but sometimes perhaps he was. He would know when to stop, nothing would get out of hand with him, and she had warned him at the beginning that lovemaking would be a commitment with her. He wouldn't want that complication, but it was unlikely they could carry on much longer in this fashion.

Every time he left her she told herself she was glad they were just friends, but that didn't stop her aching for him. She would only have to say, 'I want to stay with you,' when he asked, 'Do you want to go home?' after she'd glanced at her watch. Or move closer, or hold tighter. He would take if she offered, she knew that and each time it was harder to tear herself away.

But five weeks to the day from their first meeting their relationship changed dramatically, without her making any deliberate move. An accident was responsible, and it was a day she wouldn't forget in a hurry, because she nearly burned the house down.

It had been drizzling from early morning, grey and chilly enough for late autumn instead of summer, so there had been few customers. People had to come out to her shop, usually driving several miles, and they were unlikely to make special journeys in this weather. She had a radiant paraffin heater full on, but the shop still felt chilly, and she spent most of the morning rearranging the costume jewellery in the glass-fronted cupboards and straightening shelves of sweaters.

When the connecting door into the cottage was open the cat crept in, and curled up in front of the fire. Punch wasn't allowed in here and Judy was discouraged, but as there hadn't been a customer for hours Janna let her stay.

She was seeing Peter tonight, going to the theatre if he arrived in time, and that prospect cheered her. She was in two minds about shutting early, but if a late customer should turn up it wouldn't be fair on them, so she wandered between shop and cottage, putting out her clothes for later, laying the table for two in case they missed the theatre. There was a play on television she wouldn't mind seeing, perhaps they would stay in here. They rarely did, but it had been a dreary day and looked like being a dreary night, hardly the weather for coasting around.

When it was almost closing time she brought in paraffin in a plastic container, and a funnel, and lifted the drip-bottle out of the back of the heater. She should have turned off the fire first, and given it a few minutes to cool down before attempting to refill it. Everybody knew that, but long habit had made her foolhardy, she had been refilling heaters with the flame still burning for years.

But this was once too often, because when she had put in the bottle this morning she couldn't have screwed on the top correctly. It had stayed in place somehow, but now, as she lifted it, the top came off and the unconsumed oil poured out, igniting and flaring, so that in seconds the heater was a roaring bonfire.

She might have caught fire herself, but as she stumbled back the flames seemed to leap sidewards, touching the sleeve of a chiffon dress and flaring along the closely packed rail.

It all happened so quickly, flames, and black choking fumes as somewhere foam rubber caught. There was a fire extinguisher in the kitchen and she ran for it, sobbing with terror, her eyes streaming and smarting.

The beams were tarred and old, the white walls between were wattle. The roof was no longer thatched, but old cottages were combustible as dry tinder. The forge—the shop—was stone, but if the flames reached the cottage everything would burn.

The extinguisher was in the cupboard under the sink where it had been for years, and it might not work because she didn't know how old it was. She fell on her knees, scrabbling among buckets and paint tins, blinded by scalding tears, grabbing the little canister and rushing back through the living room.

She bumped against the table with the typewriter, sending it crashing, but she didn't stop to look, dashing for the connecting door to the shop through which the smoke was pouring.

She didn't even know how this thing worked, but she dragged at the red tag, ripped a strip of plastic from round the top and pressed down as hard as she could, and nothing happened. She was sobbing and praying, pressing the top, banging it with her fist, and suddenly spray came, a glob, then a rush of foam, and she turned it blindly where the smoke was thickest. If the flames reached the roof beams nothing could save anything.

She could hear Punch barking behind her and remembered Judy, and went into the smoke-filled room, gasping and calling, 'Judy, where are you?' Which was just about the most idiotic thing she could do, but somebody was looking after idiots that day, because the cat jumped for her, needle claws fastening into her shoulder, and Janna stumbled back out again, spraying the fire extinguisher until it was empty, then shutting the door.

The house was filling with smoke, but the door was thick. The roof beams would burn before the door, and she should have phoned the fire brigade. She should have phoned them at the beginning. She grabbed up the phone and rubbed her eyes with the back of her hand because she couldn't see the numbers for smoke and smarting tears.

She got through a call, and then she ran through the kitchen, grabbing the birdcage as she went. Judy streaked out as soon as the kitchen door opened, with Punch right behind, and Janna ran round into the lane where a woman from the cottage opposite was standing at her front door, looking up at the roof of the shop and the faint spirals of smoke.

'I'm on *fire*!' Janna screamed, and the woman screamed back, 'Have you called the firemen?'

'Yes. Just.'

'Let's get a hose on it.' The neighbour fled to fix a garden hose to her kitchen tap, unravelling it as she came down the path and across the road. There wasn't enough pressure to reach the roof, but they sprayed water on the walls as high up as they could, and in the next few minutes everyone in the village seemed to have heard the news, there was a crowd almost filling the lane.

Somebody got a ladder up and a bucket chain was formed, a man at the top throwing the water over the roof. No flames had appeared yet, but the windows were blocked solid with yellow smoke so that it was impossible to see inside.

The fire brigade arrived within ten minutes, which was good going, although it seemed to Janna that hours had passed since the oil first flared, cleared the amateurs out of the way, and went inside, wearing helmets and masks, and carrying fire-fighting equipment.

Betsy was gripping Janna's arm and Janna's jaw ached with clenching, and there they stood until the firemen told them it was all right. The fire was out and the embers were well damped down, and in the cottage the only damage had been from smoke.

Punch had been running up and down the lane, having the time of his life; Judy was up a tree, and when Betsy insisted on taking Janna home for a stiff drink, before they set foot in the cottage, Janna went round the back to see how McNaught had fared.

'The kitchen wasn't too bad, I think he was all right when I brought him out,' she babbled. 'But smoke's deadly to birds. They used to take canaries down the mines to check for gas.'

'Did they now?' Betsy was more concerned for Janna than the budgerigar, and McNaught was still on his perch, looking little the worse for his ordeal.

'Wa-ha!' he squawked as Janna picked up the cage. She said, 'Can I bring him with me? He feels the cold. He could do with more feathers.'

'Come on,' said Betsy. Janna was in a slight state of shock, and Betsy wanted to get her warm and sitting down, because there could be bigger problems waiting for her than whether McNaught had caught his death.

So far as Janna was concerned her home was still standing, and she was so deeply grateful that she was almost euphoric. She felt lightheaded with relief. 'I don't need brandy, thanks,' she said, as Betsy took the brandy bottle out of the sideboard cupboard. 'I'd rather have tea.' And as she drank tea, hot and sweet, she said, 'I thought everything was going. It would have done, wouldn't it, if that roof had been thatched?' She sagged back in her chair. 'Phew, what an escape!'

Betsy agreed that far, but she wondered how much damage had been done, and she was waiting until Andrew arrived before letting Janna go back.

Several neighbours came over. Mrs Moore, the neighbour with the hose, came within a few minutes to ask, 'Is she all right?'

'She's having a cup of tea,' said Betsy at the door of the apartment.

'There's an awful mess,' said Mrs Moore. 'We've got the doors and windows open and the smoke's clearing, but it is a mess.'

'She's a bit shaken up,' Betsy whispered. 'She doesn't realise it, but she is, and I want her to stop here until she's steadier.'

'Right,' said Mrs Moore, adding in an even lower voice, 'It's a wonder she's around to tell the tale—it must have gone up like a bomb.'

Janna, who was sitting holding her hot cup of tea, was just discovering that the backs of her hands were tender and that she must have scorched them. She was beginning to ache and smart, especially her shoulder where her sweater was stuck. She peeled it back slowly and painfully and stared at the long scarlet claw marks and the blood that had trickled and dried.

Betsy came back from the door and asked, 'How did *that* happen?'

'Judy jumped for me,' Janna explained. She sniffed her sweater. 'It smells revolting. It's the smoke, I suppose. Could I have a wash?'

'You look as though you could do with a bath,' said

Betsy, and when she saw her reflection in the bathroom mirror Janna didn't know whether to laugh or cry.

She looked as though she had been up a chimney, her face was daubed with sweat and soot, and her hair had an all-over singed frizz. In the bath her hands smarted so badly that Betsy had to sponge her down while she kept her hands above water. Even her face was sore.

She was dabbing her shoulder with ointment, and herself with a large soft towel, when Andrew returned from work, and Betsy sent him across to the cottage to assess the damage. He came back into the living room of the apartment as Janna came out of the bathroom and he said, 'You can't do anything over there tonight. I should leave it till tomorrow, there's a lot of clearing up to be done. You're lucky the fire didn't get into the cottage.'

'I know I am.' Janna was wearing one of Betsy's dresses, and she tied the belt carefully because her hands hurt. 'But I'd better be seeing it,' she said.

There were still people around, although from the outside there was nothing to see. Andrew had closed the doors after him and brought along the key. Now he opened the front door and said, 'The damage is in there,' nodding towards the shop.

It was bad enough in the living room. You could still taste smoke and everywhere looked dingy and tarnished, as though the place had been empty for years. The white walls were varying shades of yellow, and the fresh crisp muslin curtains hung limp as dirty rags.

But it was when she reached the dividing door that Janna felt faint. She couldn't believe there was one item left that would ever be saleable. Shoes and handbags were charred. Rails and shelves of blackened garments had been ruined by fire and smoke and foam. Everything was debris, a rubbish dump, and she took a few steps into the room, staring at the heater that had started it all, burned out and matt black from smoke.

She couldn't do anything here tonight, she hadn't the strength. She heard Andrew say, 'You're insured, of course?' and she shook her head and there was a shocked silence, then Betsy touched her arm and said,

'We'll start on it in the morning. It'll be dark soon and the wires should be checked before you try turning on the lights. Let's go home now.'

I am home, thought Janna, this is my home and my livelihood. But she went with them into the other room, and picked up a plate from the table, examining it as though it was valuable and might have been damaged. It wasn't and she didn't know why she was looking at it.

She put it down again and went to one of her father's paintings on the wall. Smoke had turned the glass opaque and she drew a finger down it, revealing bright colours beneath. This was the painting of the fields of wheat with the sun on them, and it seemed that all her happy childhood was in that picture.

She wanted to run into caring arms, like a child with a cut knee, and she had friends who would comfort and help, but the struggle ahead would be a lonely one.

'You can't do much tonight.' That was a neighbour. 'I'll give you a hand tomorrow.' And there was a murmur of agreement from several others who had come in.

'Thank you,' said Janna.

'You were lucky to get out,' said a man.

'She got the cat and bird out too,' said Betsy, and laughed. 'They were the only things she ran with.'

Allan was in the room, pushing across to Janna. 'Are you all right?' He held her tenderly, and she managed to smile and reassure him that she was fine. 'What a state!' he said, looking around, and the place looked dirty and derelict. The floor was covered with grubby paper like litter, and Allan swooped on one sheet with a cry of horror. 'My God, look at this!'

The table had been righted again, the typewriter

replaced on it, but nobody had bothered to pick up the papers, and the handwritten page he was holding was almost illegible. Janna had been typing from it, and Allan rushed around, gathering them all up as though they were an original Shakespearean manuscript. She said, 'I'm sorry.'

'You might have got this out instead of that damn bird!' he yelped. 'What if the place had burned?'

She hadn't thought about Allan's book, she had just thought about the living things; but if her home had burned down his papers would have been his first concern.

'Might I?' she said shortly, and he realised how everybody was looking at him and how he must have sounded.

He muttered, 'Sorry,' then, excusing himself, 'But it is the only copy.'

He had written those pages in the last few days, he had his notes, he could surely remember and write them again, she thought resentfully. He had gathered them up, a bundle he would sort out later, and he was asking solicitously, 'Is there anything I can do?'

'No, thank you,' said Janna. 'I'm going back with Betsy.'

She wanted to get away from the smell and the taste of burning. 'She'll be staying with us,' said Betsy, and the two girls went, leaving Andrew to clear everyone out and lock up again.

After seeing the shop Janna had some idea of the size of her problem, and it was overwhelming. She said, 'I think I'd better have that brandy,' and Betsy poured Janna a stiff one, with one for herself and one for Andrew.

'You're going to eat something,' said Betsy. 'Chips and omelette all right?'

Janna's stomach heaved. 'I don't think I could——' she began, and as Andrew came in, putting her front door key on the sideboard, 'Please would you leave a note upstairs for Peter, and tell him I'm here?'

'Are you seeing Peter tonight?' Betsy knew they were supposed to be going to the theatre, but Andrew didn't, and he looked relieved. 'Good,' he said. 'Do you want to write the note?'

Her hands were sore, but that wasn't why she said, 'Would you? Just say I'm here.' It was because they were trembling so badly that the writing would have been terrible. Peter would have thought she'd either aged seventy years or that she was on the edge of a breakdown. She'd be better in a few minutes, but right now, just after seeing the shop, she had the shakes.

The smell of cooking oil from the kitchen nauseated her, she was feeling sick already and she was sure she couldn't face chips and omelette. While Andrew was writing, 'Janna's down with us—Andrew,' on the back of an envelope she went into the kitchen.

Betsy was opening a bag of frozen chips and the pan of oil was beginning to bubble sluggishly. She looked round and smiled at Janna, then her smile stiffened because Janna was very pale. 'Could I lie down?' asked Janna.

'Best thing you could do,' said Betsy, and moved the pan of oil from the heated ring—she was very fire-conscious at the moment. 'The spare bed isn't made up yet, I'll do it later. You come and lie down on our bed.'

She took Janna into her bedroom, and Janna took off her shoes and lay on top of the counterpane. 'I'm being a fool,' said Janna. 'The danger's over now and now I've got the jitters. But if I could just get to sleep for ten minutes or so I'd be all right.'

Betsy pulled the curtains across the window. It wasn't dark yet, but that put the room into a restful half light. She stood by the bed for a moment and said softly, 'It will be all right. Don't you worry, when Peter comes he'll think of a way.'

A way to what? The door closed and Janna smiled. If she hadn't she might have started to weep, because what could Peter do? The law couldn't help her. She had been the negligent one, there was nobody who should be recompensing her.

Andrew thought Peter Craig had the answer to every problem. But unless Peter could turn back the clock she had a burned-out shop, and a loan she couldn't repay, and she was in trouble.

She was absolutely exhausted. She closed her eyes and lay still. She wouldn't think about it now, she could do no good thinking. But the blackened image of the shop seemed burned into her brain, and the living room—everything dirty, everything smelling sour from smoke. Her index fingertip was still stained with the grime she had rubbed from the glass covering her father's painting.

She tried to think about that painting, which was one of her favourites. She had sat on the hillside with her father when he put the first stroke on the canvas. A day of sunshine with the yellow fields of corn below. She tried to think herself back into that safe and happy past, and drifted into a relaxation that was almost sleep.

She would have fallen asleep if there hadn't been the knocking on the door. Four or five times that brought her back to sharp awareness, and each time she lay waiting to hear if it was Peter. It must have been neighbours, concerned and enquiring. There were phone calls too; they all had her straining ears and eyes, waiting for Andy or Betsy to call her or come into the room.

She had given Peter up, he was very late. They wouldn't have got to the theatre, and he might have tried to phone her but nobody was there to answer, and perhaps her phone wasn't working. He might have phoned here and said would they let her know he couldn't come. When they told him what had happened, and said that Janna wasn't hurt and she was resting now, he might have said, 'Don't disturb her, I'll ring her tomorrow.'

But she listened each time the faint knocking on the

front door reached her, and when Betsy came in and said, 'It's Peter,' she sat up with a tremendous feeling of relief.

There was nothing he could do, but she *had* wanted to see him tonight. She swung her feet off the bed. 'I'll be right in,' she said, but he was just behind Betsy demanding, 'What the hell have you been doing?'

'A little arson,' she said. 'That's all.'

Her shoes were by the bed and she pushed her feet into them as he came across the room. But when he caught hold of one of her hands she flinched with an involuntary gasp of pain, and Betsy switched on the light and Peter looked at the back of the hand, still pink under its covering of lotion.

She must be a real sight, no make-up at all and her hair all frizzled. He was looking more concerned than she had ever seen him look about anything, and she told him, 'I'm all right. I was resting. It does take it out of you, does arson.'

'Come and have something to eat,' said Betsy.

In the living room Janna sat down again on the settee, with her almost untouched glass of brandy still on the long low teak table, and Peter sat beside her. 'What happened?' He sounded grim.

Hadn't anyone told him? She said, 'An oil heater went up, in the shop.'

'But you're all right?' She wanted to go on being bright and flippant, but suddenly she couldn't get out another word. She nodded instead, biting her lip, close to tears.

Andrew said, 'It was more or less confined to the shop, but the stock's a write-off, and she wasn't insured.' He sounded apologetic, as though he hoped Janna wouldn't mind him mentioning this.

'That was stupid,' said Peter.

She knew it was, but money had been so tight after her father died that she had let the fire insurance lapse.

It had been part of the gamble, and she had never believed the worst could happen. She told Peter what Andrew and Betsy had known from the beginning, 'I got a bank loan to start the business, with the cottage as collateral.'

She had started repaying, reducing the debt, but she couldn't see how she could go on paying now and she muttered, almost to herself, 'I don't know how I'm going to manage.'

'We could probably do something about the financial position,' Peter mused, and she said quickly and huskily,

'Thank you, but I'd rather not borrow any more.' She knew as she spoke that she would have to borrow if anyone would lend to her, and she didn't want to feel like this, weak and scared and needing his help.

She sighed and he said, 'Too late for the theatre—sorry,' as though that mattered now; and she realised he was trying to make her smile.

'What were you going to see?' Andrew enquired, grinning in anticipation of his little joke. '*The Lady's Not For Burning?*'

'Very funny,' said Betsy, leaning over the back of the settee on Janna's side, glad that Peter was here and that Janna was beginning to smile.

'I've forgotten what it was now,' said Janna. The name of the play had gone clean out of her head. 'Something with a message.'

'Between ourselves,' said Peter, 'I'm not sorry to be missing it.'

'Sounds like Allan's book,' Betsy gurgled, and came round the settee to tell Peter, 'Some of that got trampled on when the firemen came, and Allan said Janna should have saved that before the bird and the cat. He said, "What would have happened if the place had burned down?" His papers, he was worried about, not the house.'

Peter chuckled, ruffling Janna's singed hair affectionately, 'You came out with the bird and the cat, of course?'

'And with Punch,' said Janna. 'We all shot out together.' It was Peter's touch, more than his offer of financial help, that seemed to support and strengthen her. She felt it light against her cheek, calming and soothing, and she turned her face into the palm of his hand and sighed, 'What a day!'

'You should see what the cat did,' said Betsy. 'No gratitude. She could be scarred for life.'

'You don't say,' said Andrew, acting intrigued.

Janna laughed, as Peter looked her over: face and arms, bare legs where Betsy's button-through dress fell away. 'Nowhere it shows,' Peter announced.

'That depends,' said Betsy with a leer, and they were all four laughing, then Peter said, 'Thanks for looking after her. We may see you later.' He stood up and seconds later Janna got to her feet. It seemed as natural she should be going with Peter as it was that Punch should follow her.

When Peter turned on the lights in the apartment the first thing to catch the eye was the white envelope propped against the phone. While Janna waited for Punch to finish climbing the stairs Peter went to the phone. He was holding the note as she and Punch came into the room.

'Note from Andrew,' he said, and as he seemed to be reading it for the first time she asked,

'How did you know where I was?'

'I went straight to your house.' He put the envelope in the pocket of his jacket and looked across at her. 'There were no lights and nobody answered. Then a woman came out of one of the cottages.' He hesitated, and she thought incredulously—he doesn't like remembering, it's an effort for him to talk about it.

He said harshly, 'She told me a fire had gone up like a bomb,' and he smiled down at her. 'Then, thank God, she told me you were over here and you were all right.'

But beneath his tan he was pale; he had cared. 'Remind me to go back for my car,' he said. 'It seemed quicker to walk than get in and back out and drive over. As a matter of fact, I ran.'

The idea of Peter running to reach her was surprising and thrilling. She had never felt as close as this to him before. Nor as safe as when he put his arms around her and sat her gently down on the green velvet armchair with a cushion behind her.

She would have preferred the settee, where he could have sat beside her, but it was comforting to have him fetch a stool and put her feet on it. 'Now I'll get you a drink,' he said.

Janna wasn't sure about that, she hadn't eaten for ages. Unless he meant a cup of tea, and he didn't, because he was pouring out of a bottle. She said, 'I left the last one, at Betsy's,'

'You'd better not leave this,' he said. 'This is the real McCoy, I don't hand this out lightly.'

It was brandy again, in a brandy glass, and she sniffed it with the expression of one transported by delight. 'Aaah!' she breathed rapturously.

'I'm glad you appreciate it.'

'To be honest,' she took a sip and it was silky smooth slipping down her throat, 'I don't know one from another. They all smell the same to me, including the stuff in the little square bottles you use for cooking.'

'You're a peasant.' He said it with a warm affection that was headier than the brandy, and she gurgled,

'Dead common—I know. There's a lot of us peasants around these parts.' She smiled up at him over the glass and it wasn't true that she didn't like him. She liked him very much, and he was kind, and the best person in the world to be with when you were in trouble.

She said, 'When I've drunk this maybe I'll stop thinking about my shop.'

'Drink it slowly,' he advised her, 'and think about how lucky you were.'

There had been the flames and all that smoke. She might not have found the door. She could have choked to death before anyone knew. She said, and her voice was a thread of sound, 'Yes, I was lucky.'

'We both were.' He raised her chin very gently, looking down at her face as though the sight of it re-assured him. 'Because there aren't a lot like you around. You're a very uncommon lady.'

Did he mean he was falling in love with her? She mattered to him, he meant that. How much, she won-dered, how much?

'And now,' he announced, 'I shall prepare us a feast.'

'Food?' she said like a fool, and he grinned,

'Anything else you fancy?'

If he had been serious the moment had gone. He had ended it, moving away from her. He was going to get a meal together, so he had done with serious talk for a while.

She said, 'Betsy tried to make me eat a fry-up. I'm not really very hungry.'

'Hard luck love, I am,' said Peter. 'Drink that slowly, you're not getting any more.'

She drank it very slowly indeed, but it wasn't the mellow old brandy that warmed her. It was the man, moving around in the kitchen, calling to her through the open door, 'Lasagne, how about that?' Or, 'I can recommend the quiche and the cheesecake.' Or talking about his journey down, and an articulated lorry that had overturned on the motorway, blocking three lanes with shattered crates of oranges, miraculously injuring nobody but causing traffic jams for miles.

Janna said, 'And nobody hurt? It *has* been a lucky day all round.' She wouldn't think about her shop, she would just luxuriate in being here and being looked after as though she was loved.

They ate at the round dining table. Soup first, pale and creamy, and she was laughing because Peter was telling her a funny story. She went on laughing a few seconds too long because she was trying so hard, and it suddenly sounded false. 'Sorry,' she said, in the silence that had fallen. 'But I can't block out my problems like you can.'

This was a personal problem and the biggest she had ever faced. The worry of what she would do tomorrow was there all the time, at the back of her mind. 'I wish I had your knack,' she said, and her smile was unsteady. 'Is it practice or were you born with it?'

'I started practising young,' he told her.

'I'll start practising now. This is *delicious*.' She took another spoonful of soup. 'Please go on talking,' she said. 'It is helping.'

Of course it was, just being with him was helping. He had such a lot of things he could talk about. While they were sitting over coffee and cheesecake he said that he was off to Paris, on business, at the end of next week; did she know Paris?

'No,' she said. 'I've had a few holidays abroad. I went to Italy and Spain, never to France. Is Paris as enchanting as they say?'

'Every bit.'

'Tell me about it.' She spooned a little more sugar in her coffee and said, 'I had some clothes with Paris labels in my shop,' and saw the rail of model gowns, as she had last seen them, looking like tattered black scarecrows. She couldn't help it. Her fingers curled into impotent fists. 'Oh dear,' she sighed. 'Oh, Peter, what am I going to do?'

'All right,' he said, 'we'll talk about it. I thought it might be better to leave business discussions till tomorrow, but why not now?'

She sat with her eyes fixed on him as though he was her only hope. She didn't want to presume on their friendship, or on anything, but he was so capable, so clever. The gaiety had dropped away from him, as though the table between them had become an office desk and she was a client seeking his professional advice. As he questioned her she felt there should be a tape-recorder turning or a secretary taking notes.

'Were your business papers in the shop?' he asked.

'No. In the living room.'

'Who do you owe money to?'

'Just the bank. Some nearly-new shops sell on percentage, but I bought outright. That's where the loan went. I had started to pay it back.'

'How much was it?'

She told him, and it wouldn't seem much to him, but it could bankrupt her. 'With the cottage as security,' she added.

'And that would be insured against fire when they made the loan?'

'Well, yes.'

'You've almost certainly broken the terms of agreement by letting the insurance lapse, and they could well call in the loan when they hear about the fire.'

The bank manager had been very nice, very helpful. He had known her father for years, and he might give her a chance to salvage what she could. Or he might decide she was no longer a viable risk. 'Do you have any other capital?' Peter was asking.

'If I had I wouldn't have needed a loan.'

'Nothing you could sell?'

'You know what's in the cottage. You know there's nothing.'

'What about your father's paintings? Would you consider selling some of them?'

Janna was almost sure that if she had asked outright he would have lent her money, but she had said she didn't want to borrow more and if there was another way she wanted him to find it. This could be a way, and although her instinctive reaction was to say, 'No,' she said instead, 'I don't think they'd be worth much. He used to sell something occasionally, but the price hardly covered the paints and canvas. Mostly he gave them away.'

Peter smiled, 'Perhaps he wasn't commercially minded,' and she had to smile too, agreeing,

'No, he wasn't very.'

'From what I've seen of those in your living room I think they could bring in a fair sum. Do you have others?'

'Quite a few.' Her father would be glad if some of his pictures could help her now.

'Shall I get a valuer down to look at them and give you an opinion?'

'Please, but I must have some left. They're all I've got of him, you see.' She could have lost them all in the fire. As it was they could be damaged and she said, 'The glass is all smoked up downstairs. I don't know what the ones upstairs are like. They're just canvases stacked in a cupboard.'

'We'll see about it tomorrow, but I think that could be your answer. Now, forget it.' His voice and his smile changed, the desk between them was a table again. They were no longer lawyer and client, they were a man and a woman who liked each other very much.

'I'll try.' Janna felt better already, now that there was a little light at the end of the tunnel and she wasn't all in darkness. She said, 'And don't forget your car. You said to remind you it's still in the lane.'

'I'd better see to it.' He got up, pushing back his chair. 'Have some more coffee, and don't go away.'

He must mean don't go down to Betsy's, there was nowhere else she might go. But she wanted to stay here. 'Don't be long,' she said.

As soon as he had gone she went into the bathroom to take a look at herself. She wished she hadn't flaked out on Betsy's bed like that, not without doing something about her appearance first. She had washed the smoke off her face but she hadn't put a thing on it, and she looked pale and peaked. She supposed she was lucky that her face wasn't scorched, when her hands were, and at some stage her hair must have been fairly smouldering. She rubbed some between fingertips and the frizzed ends rubbed away.

There were scissors in a kitchen drawer and she fetched them and trimmed what was going to be a fringe for a while, then as much as she could reach and see at the sides. Her hair had been shoulder-length, falling smoothly from a centre parting, and she was going to need a new style.

She heard Peter come in and called, 'I'm in the bathroom trying to get the frizz out of my hair.'

He appeared in the open doorway. 'How do you propose to do the back?' he enquired.

'I haven't got to that yet. I suppose you're no good at cutting hair?'

'You suppose right. May I make a suggestion?' She waited for it with raised eyebrows. 'I'd stop right there if I were you,' he said, 'and go to a hairdresser tomorrow.'

She took another look in the mirror. 'I don't think I've done too badly. My hands are still pretty stiff. But maybe it could do with the professional touch.' A cat's miaow brought her swinging round from the bathroom mirror to run into the living room. '*Judy*! Did you bring her?'

Of course he must have brought her. 'She was sitting on the back doorstep,' he said. 'Someone's put Freddy in his shed.'

'Thank you.' He had walked around the cottage for her. He had thought about old Freddy and gathered up Judy. She asked, 'May I give her some milk?'

'Of course.'

The cat lapped greedily when the saucer was put down on the kitchen floor, and watching her Janna said,

'She's had one of her lives. She was right in front of that stove, and I got the fire extinguisher out of the kitchen and you couldn't see a thing in the shop for smoke, and she was still in there and I had to go in and get her. As soon as I called her she jumped from somewhere. She couldn't have seen me, she just jumped for my voice, and she landed claws out on my shoulder and we both got out.'

She was realising now what an appalling risk she had taken, and Peter said quietly, 'If you couldn't see her how did you know where she was?'

She hadn't. The connecting door from the shop had been open all the time. Judy could have run out, she could have been anywhere. She said wryly, 'You'd have thought of that, wouldn't you, before you dashed in?'

'Oh yes,' he said, 'I'd have thought of it.' He reached for her and held her close and quietly. 'And in the meantime,' he said, 'she'd have used up her other eight lives.'

As always she felt his touch in every nerve and muscle, and tears filled her eyes. 'I look a guy,' she sniffed, 'and you should see over there. The shop's burned out, and the cottage is filthy, foul . . .'

He stroked the line between her brows, running fingertips round her temple, touching her eyelids and feeling the wetness of her tears. 'Come and be comforted,' he said, and he took her back into the living room, drawing her down beside him on the settee.

She gave a little contented sigh, nestling close. She felt blessedly safe with him, no longer alone. But she wished she felt less battered and bruised because she wanted him to love her, and when his grip tightened on her shoulder, turning her towards him, she winced.

He undid a couple of buttons, slipping the dress off her shoulder where the clawmarks still showed dark and deep. 'Judy,' she said jerkily. 'Like Betsy said—no gratitude.'

'Blind trust,' he said, and bent to kiss her shoulder.

'It jumped for your voice, and felt there was safety there.'

'Animals believe things like that.' And not only animals. She was beginning to believe that she would take a leap in the dark if Peter called her. She wanted him to go on kissing her skin until his mouth reached the softness of her breasts. She asked huskily, 'Can I stay here tonight?'

He was smiling at her, but he wasn't going on kissing her. 'Of course,' he said. 'And you can have the big bed.'

'I can?' There was a sudden aching tightness in her chest. 'Just me?'

'You need a sound night's sleep and that's the only way I can guarantee you one.'

'Well, thank you,' she said lightly. 'I'm grateful. Not flattered, but grateful. And surprised.'

He grimaced, 'I'm surprising myself, but it's been a bad day for you. You're upset and worried.'

'And not quite myself?' she said with delicate irony. 'And you're not the man to take advantage?'

He was laughing at her. 'Of course I am,' he said. 'Any advantage I can get.' Then he asked, as though her answer mattered, 'Will you come to Paris with me?'

He wasn't laughing at her. He wanted her in Paris with him and that would be wonderful. What she needed tonight was to be put to bed with a kiss and a cuddle like a child. She needed comfort and security, not passion, and Paris in just over a week's time would get her through the days between.

She would be herself by then. Paris, the city for lovers, with Peter whose lightest touch filled her with pounding sensation.

'Yes, I'll come,' she said, adding demurely with dancing eyes, 'Thank you for asking me.'

'You're welcome,' Peter said gravely.

# CHAPTER SIX

JANNA woke in the night, in the big bed, and put out a hand although she knew she was alone. The breathing she could hear was Punch, curled up somewhere on the carpet. Peter was in the other room, the guest room, the spare room, although it would have been more sense for her to have taken the smaller bed as she was about half his size.

She had protested at that, but he'd taken no notice. He had kissed her goodnight and said he would see her in the morning, and she had tried to protest again at being left in here alone.

But she was still alone. She could of course get up and wander around, needing a glass of milk or a cup of tea. He might hear her and come out, or she could knock on his door and say 'Tea up.' But at three o'clock in the morning tea might not be welcome, and neither might she. And unless she got dressed again she couldn't go on pottering around.

She had had no nightdress with her last night, and she couldn't see herself bothering Betsy to supply one, so she had ended up between the sheets wearing nothing. Probably Peter thought she always slept that way, but actually she had rather old-fashioned tastes in night attire. She wore cotton mostly, in prim and pretty styles.

It felt odd wearing nothing. It felt odd being up here, in Peter's apartment, instead of in her own little room. Yesterday's nightmare was still vivid in her mind, but she felt safe here.

In the pale light streaming through the window she could see the sweep of the dressing table where Caroline's photograph had stood. There was no photograph now.

Had Caroline taken it that Sunday, or was it in one of the drawers? All that mattered was that it had gone.

She wouldn't think about Caroline. She would think about Paris. She snuggled down again, closing her eyes and stretching from tip to toe, then relaxing into limpness.

Flying to Paris. Flying high, with Peter beside her. When she slept in her dreams she was above the clouds, and they were soft and white, and Peter was smiling at her, loving her.

She woke at the tap on the door, feeling dim and drowsy for a moment and then focusing into awareness. She sat up, pulling the sheet high under her chin, croaking, 'Come in.'

He was shaved, fully dressed, grey silk tie neatly knotted, silk shirt pristine smooth. He was carrying a cup and saucer and if she took it from him she would have to let go the sheet. It was ridiculous to be prudish about showing too much when last night she had invited herself to stay here, and when she was off to Paris with him in a few days' time. But he smiled as though he read her thoughts and put down the cup on a table by the bed.

She said, 'Thank you. What time is it?'

'Time I was away. How did you sleep?'

'Out like a light.' Most of the time she was. 'Are you really off?'

'Yes.'

Janna was annoyed at herself about that. She had meant to get up early, so that they could have had some sort of breakfast together, even if it had only been a shared pot of coffee. She wished he had called her sooner, but it seemed his main objective this morning was to be up and away.

He said, 'I'll probably be back at the weekend. Why don't you stay here until the cottage is cleaned up? There's food in the freezer and the animals seem to have made themselves at home.'

'Thank you.' That would mean she wouldn't have to bother anybody, and it would be rather fun having this splendid place all to herself.

'Bye, love,' he said, and kissed her raised face. At the door he asked, 'By the way, is your passport still valid?'

'Oh yes.'

'Good. Pack for Thursday week.'

She wanted to run across to him. There was a magnetism in the blue gaze of his eyes that could have drawn her into his arms. Her toes curled, and her fingers tightened holding the sheet. 'I'll do that,' she said, and Peter smiled at her again and was gone, and that was as well, she thought.

When she heard the outer door close she got out of bed and started to dress. She went barefoot into the living room, where Judy was still curled up on the deep green velvet chair. The cat must have spent the night there and it was too late now to shoo her off. Later the chair would have to be well brushed down.

Punch followed Janna out of the bedroom and into the bathroom. They certainly *had* made themselves at home. Punch was flopping down on the bathroom rug as though he owned the place.

It was a very luxurious bathroom, Janna would have liked to linger here, but there was too much to be done, so she settled for a wash rather than a soak, and when she heard Betsy calling, 'Yoo-hoo?' she opened the bathroom door, buttoning Betsy's dress she had borrowed last night, and tying the belt.

'It's all right,' she said, 'Peter's gone.'

'I know he has.' Betsy had let herself in with her key. 'He stopped to tell Andy something. How are you feeling?' That was a serious question, but as she asked it she began to smile.

'Much better, thank you,' said Janna, and Betsy chuckled,

'I thought Peter would take your mind off your troubles.' Automatically Betsy headed for the kitchen and started to stack last night's plates into the dish-washer. Janna had wanted to wash up last night, and when Peter overruled that she had intended to do the washing up this morning, early.

Now here was Betsy, busy in the kitchen. 'I'll make the beds,' said Janna.

'Beds?' Betsy didn't believe the plural, and when Janna said,

'Two rooms,' she said derisively,

'You're joking!'

'Take a look,' Janna invited her, and Betsy frowned, and seemed a little disappointed.

'But—— I thought——'

'However,' said Janna airily, 'I could be going to Paris with him next week.'

'Paris?' Betsy came out of the kitchen at that, to the door of the spare room where Janna was making a swift and tidy job of the bed in which Peter had spent the night.

'He's going on business, of course,' said Janna, 'but he has asked me to go along.'

Betsy liked the sound of that. 'You go,' she advised, in case Janna might be hesitating. 'You need a holiday after yesterday, and you've got a busy time coming. You go, it'll be lovely.'

'Yes,' said Janna softly, 'I think it will.'

As she tidied the bedrooms she went on talking though the open doors to Betsy in the kitchen. 'Peter said he thought my father's paintings might bring in some-thing. He's sending somebody along to look at them.'

'They might be,' Betsy called back. 'Hey, they might be worth a fortune.'

Janna was a long way from being that optimistic. 'The last one he sold fetched ten pounds, I doubt if the market's improved that much. Although Peter did say he thought it could be the answer to the money I owe the bank.'

'He should know,' said Betsy. 'He's got a couple of Picassos in his London flat.'

That was impressive. 'Wow!' said Janna, and saw herself, pale and unimpressive, in the mirror of the dressing table. A man with Picassos on his walls had style, as well as money. She was out of her league, but she was still going to Paris. She would have her lovely time, even if it didn't last. She said, 'My father was hardly Picasso.'

'No.' Betsy didn't think he was. 'What I meant was that Peter does know about pictures. If he said you'd get a good price I bet you will.' Some of the enthusiasm went out of her voice as she remembered the house last night. 'What sort of a state are they in? We'd better go and see.'

'Yes. Yes, all right.' Janna had been putting off this moment. She didn't want to see her home in the clear searching morning light, and start the dreary interminable task of dredging through the debris.

She put on her shoes and picked up the tea Peter had brought her. It was cooling by now, but she went into the kitchen sipping it. Then she swilled the cup and saucer under the tap and said, 'I bet it looks even worse this morning.' She looked around for Judy, picking the cat up from the living room floor, and Betsy gasped,

'Where did she come from?'

'Peter brought her back last night. He'd left his car over there.'

'He was in a state last night.' Betsy shut a high sliding door on neatly stacked china. 'When I said you were in bed he wanted to know what the doctor said, and when Andy said we hadn't called a doctor we were just about to get a right blast, only Andy got in quick that you were fine.'

'And so I am.' There was a lump in Janna's throat. 'Thanks to all of you.' Betsy gave a yelp of laughter.

'I was just going to say—any time. Once is enough though, isn't it? I'd say once was more than enough.' As they went out she asked, 'Will you be coming back?'

'He said to use it until the cottage was cleaned up.'

'I thought he might,' said Betsy. She beamed, 'It'll be nice having *you* upstairs.' She didn't say, 'A nice change from the last one,' but Janna knew that she was remembering Caroline.

'We've got your key,' said Betsy, slipping into her apartment to fetch it. 'Andy's gone,' she said, rejoining Janna on the stairs. 'Do you want to say good morning to McNaught?'

'Is he all right?'

'He's still squawking.'

'Is he being a nuisance?'

'No. I'll bring his seed back,' said Betsy. 'After you saved him from the fire it would be a shame if we lost him from undernourishment.' She went on chattering, 'Not a bad day.' The sun was trying to break through clouds and there was a fresh breeze. 'But nothing to write home about considering it's midsummer.'

As they crossed the green Janna put Judy down. She had carried her, stroking her in absent-minded fashion until then. Judy trotted ahead, towards home, and with the dog at their heels the two girls reached the bottom of the lane.

The board 'Janna's Place' hung apparently unmarked, and Betsy's chatter died away. She had been trying to cheer up Janna, but she felt sick at heart herself. She had helped to build up that little business, and loved doing the sewing and making the alterations. She had taken an expensive suit back yesterday morning, after taking in the side seams, but the customer hadn't collected it when the fire started. Betsy wished now that she had made the job last longer, although one garment saved wouldn't have made much difference.

Neither girl spoke, but they kept very close together

on the narrow pavement, shoulders brushing. The window in the shop was cracked, all the windows were dirty. Those were the only external signs of fire, but when Betsy tried to put the key into the lock she fumbled and dropped it.

Janna picked it up and gave Betsy a wan grin. 'Not much to choose between us,' she said. 'Let's get cracking. We'll feel better once we get started.'

The smell that reached them when she opened the front door was still pungent enough to sting at the back of the nose. She left the door open and went through into the kitchen to open the back door, while Betsy pulled back the latches on the living room windows and pushed them ajar.

There was an open staircase from the living room, leading to the three bedrooms, and Janna went up. One bedroom door had been open and the walls in there were badly smoke-stained. It had been her father's room, only used for the occasional guest since his death. The middle room was a boxroom, and in her own bedroom only a little smoke had crept past the ill-fitting old door.

On the bed were the clothes she had put out to go to the theatre with Peter. Like everything else they smelt fusty, but her father's canvasses in the big floor-to-ceiling cupboard hadn't suffered at all.

Janna breathed a prayer of thanks for that. Less for the money they might bring than because she could keep some of them, and they were the most precious things she had because of the man who had painted them.

'All right?' Betsy was calling from the bottom of the stairs.

'Not bad. The pictures weren't touched.'

Betsy was holding the phone, which stood on a little table near the stairs. 'This seems O.K.', she said as Janna clattered down. 'I'm getting the dialling sound. Do you think we'd better ring for an electricity check? You don't want another fire.'

'Would you?' said Janna.

Punch was snuffling around, bewildered by the new odour that masked every familiar smell. He came across to Janna and stayed close, fearful that she too might be overtaken by this change.

As Betsy began to dial Janna went into the shop, and last night's fears were confirmed. It was a dead loss. Drawers and cupboards might have been some protection, but everything on the shelves and racks was black and sodden. The only thing to do was clear everything out, and as she stood there, wondering where to start, she heard Mrs Moore behind her asking, 'How are you this morning?'

'Better than this place,' she said sadly.

Mrs Moore turned back to the living room, which was less depressing than the shop. 'This won't be so bad once it's got a fresh coat of paint on it,' she said encouragingly. 'I'll give you a hand with the cleaning, and Peggy said she'd be over as soon as she's got the children off to school.'

Peggy was another neighbour, all the neighbours were being kind. Mrs Moore was quite enjoying herself. She had known Janna from a small child, and she felt a personal interest in the fire. If it hadn't been for her hose the flames might have taken a firmer hold, and she was the one who had broken the news to Peter Craig too. That would be something to discuss with all the women who were wondering about that affair.

She said, 'I told Mr Craig where to find you.'

'Thank you,' said Janna.

'When I told him what had happened he said, "Where is she?" and I said she was at your place'—nodding at Betsy. 'Very surprised he was.'

'Who wasn't?' said Betsy.

Allan came around before he drove off to school, and explained that he had been over to Betsy's first, wasting a good five minutes. He'd be in again as soon as school was through, he said, and he shook his head as though he was seeing everything for the first time.

'Bring a bucket and scrubbing brush when you come tonight,' said Janna.

'Won't the insurance folk want to see it first?' asked Allan. 'To assess the damage?'

'I'm not insured.' Both Allan and Mrs Moore made shocked little noises at that. 'I think I'll get the stuff out of the shop first,' she said. She didn't need anybody else telling her she had been improvident, and sympathy wouldn't clean any walls. She needed some action, and there was plenty of scope here for that.

'Goodbye,' she said to Allan, and he kissed her cheek and she went off and let Freddy out of his shed. It was no effort to move away from Allan, there was no magnetic pull there. When he heard that she was going to Paris with Peter that could be the end of their friendship, and this time yesterday that would have worried her. But nothing again was going to be exactly the way it was yesterday.

Her little world had suffered an upheaval, as traumatic and unexpected as a terrorists' bomb on a passer-by. She was lucky to be alive and she was taking what happiness she could get. For a while at least.

She put on rubber gloves, her hands were still tender, and she and Betsy started to clear out the shop. There was a back door that hadn't been opened for years, but they hammered back bolts that had been painted over, and the blistered paint flaked away. The hinges creaked and the door opened, and they carried out metal racks and the long splintered cheval mirror, the charred remains of the wooden chest that had stood under the window, and a small table and a couple of chairs.

A pile of blackened clothing was heaped in the little yard, and the pile grew higher while the box, into which they dropped anything that might be salvaged, remained almost empty.

Mrs Moore and Peggy worked like stalwarts. Mrs Moore swabbed down walls and ceilings with a long-handled mop, while Peggy took away curtains and chair covers and bedding to wash. She left some on her own clothes line, and brought back a basket full to flap between two trees in the paddock. The wind was brisk, it was a good drying day, and the sheets didn't seem to bother Freddy, who spent most of his time with his head over the fence watching the clearing out of the shop.

They broke off for lunch, and after lunch there was a change of helpers, although Mrs Moore continued to supply hot water, carried over in slopping buckets from her cottage opposite.

The man from the electricity board turned up during the morning and announced that the shop needed completely rewiring. Everything must be disconnected until the damaged wires were repaired and they couldn't start on that until next week.

'Ah well,' shrugged Janna, who wouldn't have been surprised to have her whole circuit condemned.

There was a phone call from Peter's secretary. She didn't give a name. As soon as she was assured that she was speaking to Miss Joanna Wyman she said, 'This is Peter Craig's secretary.' She had an attractive voice and Janna could imagine her, sophisticated and ultra-efficient, in the London office. Peter wanted Janna to know that a Mr Harry Bush would be along tomorrow afternoon to see the paintings, if that was convenient.

Oh yes, it would be convenient, Janna said, and thanked her. Then she repeated the message for Betsy, and asked if Betsy had ever met Peter's secretary.

This was during the lunch break, when Mrs Moore and Peggy had gone home to see about midday meals for their families, and before the afternoon shift of helpers had arrived. Betsy and Janna were drinking oxtail soup out of a vacuum flask, and there was nobody else around. If they had not been alone Janna wouldn't have shown so much curiosity, nor so much relief when Betsy said, 'I've never met her, but I know she's married and she's got a son at Aston University.'

'Happily married, I hope,' said Janna.

'I think so.' Betsy poured out another half mugful of soup each, emptying the flask, and picked up her mug and looked at the pattern on it. 'But she could be crazy for Peter for all I know. She wouldn't be the only one.'

She was reminding Janna that there would always be competition there, and Janna said, 'Present company excepted, *I'm* not crazy for him. I like him very much, that's all. And I like the idea of a few days in Paris next week, but I know there'll be another Caroline along one of these days. I'm not stupid enough to be falling in love with him.'

'Of course you're not,' said Betsy. She finished drinking her soup and asked, 'What are you going to do about your hair?'

Janna's hair had been discussed during the morning. The singeing had impressed them, showing how near she had been to going up in flames. But her attempts at styling had met with criticism.

'I don't know that I like you with a fringe,' said Mrs Moore. 'You've never had a fringe before, have you?'

Peggy, who had also known Janna all her life, said that she'd always liked it the way it was, and added encouragingly that it would soon grow again. But Janna wanted to look good by the weekend, and if possible devastating by the time she caught that plane. She said now, 'I'm going to the hairdressers, of course.'

'When?' asked Betsy.

'As soon as I can.'

'Why don't you go this afternoon? We'll carry on with the cleaning up, but I think you'd feel better for it.' Both girls were grubby, but Janna's hair was frizzed and spiky and Betsy gurgled, 'You do look a freak! Let me phone up, I'm sure they'd fit you in.'

Janna usually washed her own hair, it had been an easy style, falling naturally from the centre parting, but Betsy had a regular weekly appointment at a salon in a nearby village, and the woman who ran it said if she brought her friend along in about an hour they'd do a restyle and conditioning for her.

'You might have told her what happened,' Janna protested when Betsy replaced the phone, and Betsy grinned.

'She'll find out soon enough. If she'd known what a challenge it's going to be she might not have been so obliging.'

Betsy dropped Janna outside the salon and drove back again to the cottage. When Janna entered the pretty little pink-and-white shop a blonde girl came smiling to meet her, and seated her in front of one of the mirrors with a pink gingham check cape over her shoulders.

'Restyling, Mrs Byers said,' said the girl. She took a closer look and asked, 'What *have* you been doing?'

'Would you believe setting fire to myself?' said Janna, and the other hairdresser, and a customer who was having her rollers taken out, both turned to stare at her.

So she explained, and they said how dreadful it was, and how lucky she'd been, and the blonde girl feathered off the singed hair, leaving her with a shorter style with a slight flip. Washed and conditioned it shone healthily again, and Janna said to the girl, who was holding the hand mirror for her to see the back, 'I think you've done wonders for me,' and she thought—I hope Peter likes it.

She must not get into the habit of needing Peter's approval, but of course she hoped he liked her new hairstyle.

'I think I like it better than the way it was,' said Betsy when she picked Janna up, and the two neighbours who were at work in the cottage when they got back both agreed. It helped, and so did the progress they had made in the clearing up in just one day. So did everyone's kindness.

Allan came across as soon as he got home again. The women who had been cleaning upstairs were about to leave, and he exchanged a few remarks about the difference between this morning and now.

'Somebody's been hard at it,' he observed.

'Thank you very much,' Janna was saying. Goodness knows there was a great deal still to be done, but with Betsy's help she was beginning to believe that redecorating the cottage shouldn't take more than a few days.

The shop would be tougher. In there paint was blistered on the walls and the scorch marks were deep. The ceiling was black with smoke, and too high to reach easily. The shop had been cleared by the end of the afternoon, and a few pieces of costume jewellery were about the only undamaged items. The rest was waiting to be carted away in the refuse collection.

'Shall I get us a cup of tea?' Allan suggested.

'The electricity's off,' said Janna. 'There's some rewiring to be done.'

'I'll get you one back at home, then,' Allan offered. 'We could go round to the pub and eat.'

Janna didn't want sociable company tonight. She didn't feel equal to the enquiries and the condolences she would get if she took her evening meal in the crowded bar of the village inn. 'Not me,' she said, 'I just want to crawl away, get into a bath, and then drop into a chair.'

'Is she going back with you?' Allan asked Betsy, and Janna said,

'I'm staying in Peter's apartment.'

After a moment Allan said, 'Is he there?'

'Not till the weekend,' said Janna.

'Will you be staying there then?'

She could sleep in her own bedroom any time, if she used an oil lamp, but this had left her nervous about oil lamps. 'I don't know,' she said, and added because he had to be told and she might as well get it over with, 'He's going to France on business next week and I'm going too for a few days.'

'Oh,' said Allan. As the implications of that sank in the muscles of his face locked. 'There isn't much else to be said, then, is there?' he shrugged, and stalked out of the house, leaving Janna feeling sorry she had hurt him but unable to call after him.

'He took that calmly enough,' said Betsy.

'Yes.'

'Probably gone to write about it,' said Betsy with a touch of malice. From what she'd read of Allan's work she didn't think he was a genius, so she resented him carrying on as if he was. It was all right him coming round now and offering to make cups of tea, but he hadn't been much help last night. All his concern had been for his papers, getting dirty and trodden on. He'd probably spent the evening cleaning them up.

Janna stayed behind for about half an hour, after Betsy left to get a meal ready for Andrew and for herself and Janna. The cottage still felt strange and looked stark. Curtains and chair covers and bedding were clean and ironed and folded on a bed upstairs. The pictures from the walls were upstairs too. Ornaments and knick-knacks had been put into cupboards to be washed, and replaced after the rooms had been redecorated.

It was like a house you were just moving into, or leaving. Not the home where you were born. Janna told herself again how lucky she was that it was standing at all, and went to pack an overnight case with some clothes for tomorrow. These had been hanging outside all day and the fresh air had almost blown away the smell of smoke.

She walked with Freddy round the paddock, because he expected her to. She did that most nights when work was over. Judy had vanished for the moment but the cat wouldn't be far away, and would probably be happy enough tonight in the kitchen, on her usual chair. Janna would come back later to check on Judy; she took Punch with her across to the Old Vicarage and Betsy and Andrew's apartment.

Over supper they told Andrew about the man who was coming tomorrow to value the pictures, and he agreed with Betsy that if Peter had said they should fetch a good price they probably would. It cheered Andrew up. It sounded a perfect solution. 'Then as soon as you get the place redecorated you can start again,' he said.

'Just like that,' said Betsy. She knew how hard Janna had worked, building up her stock and her business. She would do it again, but the slog could be even more grinding the second time around.

'It could be worse,' agreed Janna. 'I still have a house, and if the pictures pay off perhaps the bank will let me keep it.'

'No danger there,' said Andrew heartily. 'No danger at all,' and he hoped there wasn't.

As soon as the meal was finished and cleared away Janna took up her case, leaving it just inside the door, then went over to the cottage again. As she walked through the dark little house, to open the back door and call Judy, she knew that she couldn't leave the cat here. This wasn't home any more. It was cold and inhospitable. When the paint was bright, and you could turn on the lights again, it would once more be the safe, warm, happy house she had loved. But tonight she picked up the cat and said, 'Another home for us tonight,' and carried her over to the Old Vicarage.

She had Betsy's key, but she noticed the key on the table by the phone, where Peter must have left it for her, as she walked in. Punch padded to the kitchen as though he knew his way around, and the cat followed him.

Janna had wanted to come here. She didn't realise how much until she closed the door, and walked to pick up her key and felt the aching knotted tightness leaving her. When she first came into Peter's apartment—with Betsy when she was going to cook that dinner for Caroline and the Laurences—she had thought it was too much like a contemporary magazine setting to be comfortable. 'What the New Designers Are Doing.' But now she kicked off her shoes and looked around the beautiful room and at the closed doors—all but the kitchen door that Betsy had left a little ajar this morning.

She didn't feel alone. She called, 'Hello, I'm home,' because she felt as though Peter was here, in one of the other rooms, although she knew he wasn't.

She went into the room where she had slept last night and asked, 'Which bed do I have tonight?' Then she said, 'Oh, all right, but it is a very big bed, there's a lot of space wasted.' And she laughed at herself, and flopped on the bed and said, 'I'm shattered, do you feel up to running me a bath?'

She ran her own bath, and had a lovely time, pretending she lived here. She sniffed all the lotions in the bathroom cupboard and tipped in a generous slosh of the one she liked best.

It *felt* as though Peter was here. Janna could almost believe she heard him moving around in the living room, and when she came out of the bathroom he seemed to be in the kitchen, or in one of the bedrooms. Always just out of sight, but near enough to hear when she spoke to him.

She was having an early night, but she spent a little while sitting in the turret watching the lights of cars passing below, and the steady glow of windows. Except for the church tower this was the highest outlook in the village, the nearest to the clouds.

When the phone rang she ran to it, quite sure it was for her and that Peter was calling. He was. He was glad she was there, he said, and she said gaily, 'I wasn't turning down the offer of a luxury apartment. We're all here, do you mind? Punch and Judy and me.'

'Not Freddy?'

She giggled. 'Nor McNaught. He's lodging at Betsy's for the time being.'

'How's the cottage looking?'

'Oh, we had a lot of help today. Given time I think I can fix it. With a few gallons of paint and a long strong stepladder.'

'Good,' he said. 'You'll be around to see Harry Bush tomorrow?'

'Oh yes. When do we see you again?'

He told her that he didn't think he could make the weekend and her spirits sank, but she managed not to sound too disappointed. 'Pity,' she said, and went on to tell him, 'I had my hair cut today. You wouldn't know me.'

'I'd know you,' he said, and she supposed that was a compliment. She said, 'Thank you,' anyway, and they talked a little longer before they said goodnight. About what still needed doing at Janna's Place, and Peter advised her to see her bank manager tomorrow and put him in the picture.

Janna went to bed right after the phone call and fell asleep without too much trouble. But she woke again in the night and heard an owl hooting, and remembered Caroline talking about strange nocturnal country noises. And she shivered under the warm sheets, because it was in this bed that Peter's arms would have gone around Caroline if anything woke her and scared her.

She wondered if Peter ever thought about Caroline these days. Caroline had had a key, might still have it. If Peter's affairs lasted an average of six months and he was thirty-four there must be quite a list. She wondered what number she was. It was horrid to think of herself as a number, a statistic, and this time it took her longer to fall asleep . . .

\*

Tomorrow's priorities were first phone the bank manager and fix an appointment, for after Harry Bush had been this afternoon if possible; and then sort out the pictures to await Mr Bush's verdict.

There were eighteen canvasses in the upstairs cupboard, and Betsy and Janna took them out, and washed the glass of the pictures that had been framed and hanging downstairs. 'Lucky they had glass in,' said Janna. 'I'm not selling this one.' That was the wheatfields, and she put aside another couple.

Her father had been a scenic artist, concentrating on local landscapes, and by the time all his pictures were propped up against the walls, or standing on dressing table and chest of drawers, it looked like a one-man exhibition.

'Well, I think they're super,' said Betsy. She and Andrew had a sunset scene that Janna's father had given them on their first wedding anniversary. It hung in their bedroom and she said now, 'I didn't realise there were so many. Why didn't you try to sell some of them before?'

'I didn't know who to sell them to,' Janna admitted. 'He painted because he loved painting. But they didn't sell very well.'

She was frankly nervous about this dealer Peter was sending along; and when the Volvo estate car drew up outside, and the man with the smooth dark hair and the pointed beard, looking every inch the art expert, stepped out, she found herself breaking into a cold sweat. If he said that her father's paintings were worthless she would feel like hitting him over the head.

She couldn't tell from his expression. She took him upstairs and he walked slowly round the little room, pausing for a moment or two in front of each, and she couldn't tell because his expression never changed and he never said a word.

Until he had looked at every one and then he asked, 'Do you want me to put a price on them?'

So they did have some commercial value. 'Please,' she said huskily, and he began to move around again, touching a dozen canvasses in all, and in each case stating a figure that was no fortune, but combined they came to a tidy sum. Enough to hold off the bank manager, unless he was in a very unco-operative mood.

Betsy did a jig of triumph when Mr Bush drove away, leaving a cheque and with the canvasses in the back of his car. 'Take that to old Buxton,' she said. 'If you give him that he'll surely let you have time to get things together.'

Old Buxton was the bank manager, and not so old as all that. He had been a contemporary of Janna's father, and he gave her a little lecture about letting the fire insurance lapse. But not until he had said that she had been extraordinarily lucky in getting out unscathed, and that it must have been a very nasty ordeal for her.

The interview went well. She was to pay off part of the loan, and get the shop and the cottage insured again as soon as the repairs were done, but she was even left with a little in her account. If she worked like crazy she could be open for business-as-usual as soon as she got back from Paris.

For a little while she would have to sell by taking a percentage instead of buying outright, but the main aim was to keep going so that her customers didn't drift away.

She and Betsy concentrated on the shop for the rest of that week. They got help, but not from Allan. There was no sign of Allan. Nor of Peter.

Peter phoned on Friday evening to confirm that he couldn't get down to the village over the weekend. Nor did he expect to see Janna next week, until Thursday. Work was hectic he said, but he had her plane and hotel bookings, and would she meet him in front of the Arrivals board at Heathrow at nine-thirty Thursday morning?

She would have liked to see him before then. It would

have been pleasant if they could have travelled down together, because now she would have to get to London by train. After a moment she said, 'Well, all right,' and told him about the bank manager. He knew about Harry Bush, and he said he was sorry about the weekend.

That was life. Peter's life. There was nothing she could do about it, and as she put down the phone she reflected that he must be pretty confident about her turning up. Well, maybe she wouldn't. But after this week she needed a reviver. Thursday till Sunday in Paris should boost her spirits and her stamina, so she would go. Besides—and there was no point in deluding herself—she very much wanted to be with Peter.

The phone rang again on Saturday evening. Janna and Betsy were watching the television in Peter's apartment because downstairs Andrew was watching sport, and Janna got up to answer it, giving the number.

'Is Peter there?' said the girl's voice, and Janna began to say, 'No, I'm sorry, he isn't,' but she only got as far as 'No' before the phone went dead.

She said to Betsy, 'That sounded like Caroline.'

'What did she want?' asked Betsy, although the call had been too brief for any talking.

'Peter,' said Janna, 'and I don't really know who it is.'

But she knew next day when Caroline turned up. The morning service church bells had woken Janna, and she was wandering around in the kitchen still fuzzy with sleep, when there was a knock on the door and Punch started barking.

Caroline stood there, cool in a cream cotton dress, raising cool eyebrows as she asked, 'Peter up yet?'

Janna found herself flushing, stammering, 'He isn't here.'

'Oh?' Caroline's little smile made her cheeks burn even hotter. 'Still, I'm sure he wouldn't mind. I left a bracelet behind, may I get it?'

She walked in, across to the bedroom, with the

unmade bed and Janna's clothes around. Some of Janna's make-up was on the dressing table and Caroline picked up a perfume atomiser and squirted her wrist and sniffed. It was a well-known, reasonably priced brand, and Caroline didn't seem to care for it. 'You've moved in, have you?' she said.

Janna was very conscious of her housecoat-over-nightdress, of her bare feet and ruffled hair. 'I had a fire at my cottage,' she said. 'There's no electricity at the moment.'

'How sickening for you,' drawled Caroline.

'I'm only here temporarily,' explained Janna.

'But of course you are.' Caroline opened a drawer that looked empty until she reached to the back and brought out the bracelet. It was heavy and it could have been gold, with Chinese symbols incised on it. She clasped it on to her wrist and held up her arm. 'Like it?' she said.

'It's very pretty,' said Janna.

Caroline turned her arm slowly and Janna wondered what the symbols meant. 'A gift from Peter,' she said. 'The first time he made love to me.'

It was stupid that that should hurt so badly. Janna knew that Caroline and Peter had been lovers, everybody knew, but hearing the words made her feel gaspingly sick.

Caroline must have heard the quick intake of breath, but she didn't look at Janna. She was looking at the bracelet and she sounded almost as though she was talking to herself. 'I suppose a psychiatrist would say I left this behind on purpose. I didn't want to leave it, but I did. I took my photograph and left my bracelet.' She had been wearing the bracelet on the photograph, Janna remembered now. 'And perhaps I thought it might remind him and he might return it.' She looked up and said almost gaily, 'But he didn't and I want it, so here I am come to collect it.'

Janna heard herself ask, 'Did you love him?'

'I think so.' Caroline was neither embarrassed nor

annoyed. 'Yes, I think he'd have suited me. He's against marriage and I'm not hooked on it myself, but yes, I'd have given it a try if he'd asked me. It might not have worked out, but it need not have been a life sentence.'

She laughed, as though something in Janna's expression amused her. 'And don't you get breaking your heart over him, because there is no way at all that any woman is ever going to break his.'

In the living room she went to the turret window and waved, and a car hooted below. 'I'm coming,' she called. Then, to Janna, 'If you've got any more boy-friends keep them on ice. You'll be needing them.'

When she was alone Janna moved to the window, and saw the car down there, among the churchgoers' cars. A man was standing beside it. She saw Caroline hurrying over to him, and both of them got into the car and drove away.

She wondered who she herself would run to afterwards. Standing here, in his apartment, it seemed that Peter had always been around and always would be. She knew their affair wouldn't last, that it would be exciting and highly enjoyable, and only take up a small part of her life, but somehow she couldn't imagine afterwards.

# CHAPTER SEVEN

JANNA had her last phone call from Peter, before their trip to Paris, on Monday evening, when she told him about Caroline's visit on Sunday.

'Oh?' He didn't sound very interested.

'She came to collect a bracelet she'd left behind.'

'A bracelet?' he echoed, and she said tartly,

'Covered in Chinese symbols, and from what she said it should have been quite a message.'

'Yes.' He knew the bracelet, he knew what Caroline had been talking about, but he wasn't discussing it. He went straight into the details of Thursday again, recapping where and when she was to meet him, giving her the name of the hotel where they would be staying. He could have been briefing one of his staff. Even when he said, 'You will be there?' his voice seemed more like an employer's than a lover's.

It wasn't too good a line, crackling interference was making it hard to hear and probably distorting his voice, but he didn't seem to have much to say. Janna said, 'They're doing the rewiring in the shop tomorrow.'

'Good.'

'I've seen to the insurance.'

'Yes.'

'You sound tired. Or is it busy?'

'A little of both.'

'I won't keep you, then.' He didn't try to keep her talking, she had the impression that she was not getting all his attention. When she said, 'Goodnight,' he said, 'Goodnight, love,' and that sounded to her as though he would then turn back to papers on his desk. Not to another woman, or he would hardly have called her love, but his work had been the rival of every other woman in his life.

Janna was tired too. She went to bed after that phone call. Tomorrow the electricity might be on again in her cottage, and during the weekend she would give Peter back his key. By then there would be no real excuse for her staying here any longer. The cottage would still be smoke-stained, but she would get down to painting it during the evenings.

She couldn't live here indefinitely, even when he wasn't using the apartment himself. Times had changed in the last few years. Going away on holiday together was O.K. now, but moving in to live here would raise a flurry of local gossip.

Besides, she had a perfectly good home of her own. Besides, this had never been offered as anything more than a temporary refuge.

By Wednesday the lights were on again and the shop was smelling of new paint. The metal racks had been cleaned and scoured, a set of shelves bought from a second-hand furniture shop, and painted white to match a little table and two small straight-backed chairs. There was a long mirror—also from the second-hand shop—plugged to the wall, and what was needed now was something to sell.

There had been phone calls and promises almost every day as news of the fire reached customers and friends, and Janna had phoned a couple of local papers with an advertisement that would appear on Friday and Saturday. 'Janna's Place, Lower Egginton, Nearly-New Fashion. S.O.S. Old and new customers please help me stock up again. A fire last week cleaned me out, but I shall be open for business again on Monday, and I look forward to seeing you.'

On Wednesday she did her packing for her holiday. Peter had seen all the outfits she was taking. She had worn them all on dates with him, and if the shop had still been stocked she would have treated herself to something new. They had been in her bedroom wardrobe, safe from the fire and the smoke, and she chose a grey pleated skirt and a scarlet tunic top for travelling, with scarlet sandals.

The skirt hung over a chair in her own bedroom, the tunic on a hanger behind the door, and she wasn't going back to Peter's apartment tonight. Tomorrow morning Andrew would give her a lift to the station before he went into the office, and she would get on a train to meet Peter·in London.

Whenever she thought about that her mind started whirling. She tried to act cool. Of course she was looking forward to her holiday, off to Paris for three days with a very attractive companion. She took the curiosity, and the teasing, and the frank envy with a smile, but inside she was quaking. She felt like a very young girl, all longing and apprehension, instead of a woman of nearly twenty-two. She wasn't sure about anything except that the thought of being with Peter, letting him love her, was with her every hour of the day and night.

On Wednesday evening Allan turned up, for the first time since the day after the fire. He knocked on the front door, instead of walking round the back, giving a touch of formality to his call. She was pleased to see him, and when he asked, 'How's it going?' she said,

'Come and see. The shop's ready for use again.'

He followed her to the connecting door. 'It does look rather bleak,' she admitted, 'but on Monday I'll have some rugs down and some flowers around, and I'll start getting some stock in.'

He was sure she would. She could manage without him easier than he was managing without her. He had regretted giving up so easily, he had missed Janna looking after him, and he said, 'I came to say—have a good holiday.'

She was touched; that seemed generous on his part.

'Well, thank you,' she said.

'And that I'll be here when you get back.' Waiting for her, he meant, which was more than generous and made her feel guilty and uncomfortable. She chewed on her lip as she said,

'Yes, well, thank you again,' but as he kissed her cheek she drew back instinctively so that the kiss skidded.

'It's Midsummer madness,' he said. 'You'll see.'

'You think so?'

'Who's looking after the animals?'

Allan didn't like the animals. She said, 'Betsy. Punch is staying over there.' Punch was growling very softly, watching Allan.

'I'd even have come and fed him' said Allan glumly, and that made Janna smile. She was glad they were talking again. 'How's the book?' she asked, but when he offered,

'Shall I fetch this chapter over for you to read?' she said hastily,

'Not tonight, I've got so much to do tonight,' and she decided against giving him a cup of coffee. He was looking sorry for himself, and if he started telling her about his work he could still be here very late, and she could be cooking his supper.

'You'll have to excuse me,' she said, 'but I am awfully busy right now.'

'Have a good holiday,' he said again, being edged towards the door.

When the door closed Punch wagged his tail for the first time, and Janna had to  laugh at the thought of Allan coming over to the cottage each night to feed Punch. 'It would have been water and hard tack for you, my lad,' she said.

Until she fell asleep she was listening for the phone, wondering if Peter might ring. She hadn't told him she would be back in the cottage tonight, but if he rang the apartment and got no answer he would surely realise she was here. She had been expecting another call ever since Monday, although everything had been arranged and she knew he would be waiting for her at the airport. He didn't phone, so he wasn't lying awake tonight thinking of tomorrow night.

It was late when she fell asleep and she woke again before the alarm clock went off, and got up early and forced herself to eat a cooked breakfast although she was queasy with nerves, full of little aches and tensions.

She would be all right as soon as she reached Peter, but she wished Betsy had been travelling up to London with her this morning, for a day's shopping. She would have liked someone to chatter with, and when Andy rapped on the door she dashed out, carrying her small case.

'Thanks a lot,' she said, because taking her to the station was taking Andrew a little out of his way. His office was in the town centre and the station on its outskirts. 'I really must learn to drive,' she said.

Betsy had her own little car, but Janna had caught a bus to work in the old days, and now her business came to her. One day she would get round to taking lessons and hunting for a car, but she couldn't see that happening for a long time.

Andy agreed with her that she ought to be driving, and they went along in the stream of motorists on their way to work, listening to the news on the radio. They were nearly at the station when Janna asked, 'Do you know what work Peter will be doing in Paris?'

Andrew wouldn't have discussed the details if he'd known them, but he said, 'I don't, no. But he's the solicitor for this firm. They've got branch offices over here, but the head office is Paris. He sits in on board meetings and deals with International Law points. You know the kind of thing.'

Janna laughed. 'Oh yes,' she said, 'I'm really up on international law,' and Andrew grinned.

Cars were stopping in a row in front of the station, while men mostly, chauffeured by wives, jumped out. 'What will you do with yourself while Peter's working?' Andrew asked, reaching into the back seat for her case, and Janna said,

'What a question, in Paris! There'll be lots of things to see. And lots of walking. Budgets don't come much tighter than mine.'

She was going to insist on paying her own expenses, which she could ill afford, and there wasn't going to be much spending money left, so during the day she would do a lot of walking.

It was an express train, hurtling along, full of commuters and shoppers, none of whom she knew; and she sat reading her travel book on Paris and rushing towards Peter. And no transport could have got her there fast enough.

He was waiting. She was a few minutes early and she was glad he was already there. She didn't exactly run, but she went to him quickly and he hugged her close, both arms around her, while sheer delight filled her. Everything was wonderful. Sometime in Paris she was going to fall helplessly in love with this man because he felt so good and smelt so good, and standing here with his arms around her she was so wildly happy.

'I like your hairstyle,' he said.

'Thank you,' she said, 'and I like yours.'

Peter carried his briefcase on to the plane. The holiday had started for her, but it was a working holiday for him. There was talking, and silences, as they sat side by side, high over the clouds. Janna told him everything that had happened since she saw him last, and took the apartment key out of her handbag and gave it back to him.

'I can live in the cottage again now,' she said. 'I loved your apartment, but the cottage is almost all right again now.'

He didn't say, 'Keep the key,' although it must be a

spare. He dropped it in his pocket as though it was a box of matches she was returning, and she was sorry to see it go.

He listened to her. Sometimes he talked to her. But when the silences fell he retreated into the faraway places in his mind, and at last he asked, 'Do you mind?' and took down the briefcase. She said,

'Of course not,' and he opened the briefcase and Janna looked out at the clouds.

If it had been a clear day she would have seen a fascinating panorama. But the clouds were like an unending snow plain with sunshine and blue skies above, and most times she looked at Peter he smiled at her. Not always. Sometimes he kept his eyes on the papers on his knee.

She wouldn't be really close to him until they were alone and she mustn't resent those papers, nor the hours he must spend away from her, because they would be together tonight. He would be a wonderful lover, she was sure of that, and she ached for him now. She wanted to hold his hand, or touch his face, or just say, 'Later,' very quietly, and make him look at her and smile.

But his mind was on those papers, so she said, 'Later,' to herself, silently, so that his train of thought was not disrupted.

He sounded regretful when he said he had to leave her in the hotel room. The kiss was a hurried goodbye kiss, because somewhere people were waiting for him, and Janna stood by the window telling herself that six o'clock this evening would soon come.

She had known Peter had business matters to deal with. She was here on those terms, and it was going to be wonderful. It *was* wonderful. This room was fabulous. She had wondered what this room would be like. It had been a misty background to her dreams ever since she had known she was coming to Paris.

The walls and carpet were in pale apricot, and the apricot quilted bedspread had a valance of bright yellow.

She stroked the silk bedspread and her fingers trembled. The room looked as warm as though it was bathed in sunshine, it *was* warm, but there was a chill inside her. She had thought that the flight here would have been more exciting, more *fun*. Peter could have sat with his arm around her, and read his wretched papers like that if he had to read them.

Of course he had to read them. She was too tense, that was her trouble. But how dreadful it would be if she had come here with a stranger. Peter attracted her like no other man before. She had never known what it was to want a man like this. He made her laugh, and he helped her when she needed help. But with those papers in his hand he could have been a stranger sitting beside her.

She began to unpack, taking her time about putting her few day clothes into the wardrobe, lingerie and nightdress into a drawer. She would take a walk, following her tourists' map of Paris. She would pass the time happily enough until Peter came back this evening. By then she would have shaken off her depression and she would go into his arms as she had at the airport, with wings on her feet.

His case had been put down by hers, a dark brown lightweight case for air travel. Locked, she supposed, but she didn't try the locks. She didn't feel she should be unpacking for him. He was used to doing that for himself, deftly of course, without fuss, remembering exactly where he was putting everything.

She was in no great hurry to go out. This was a lovely room and in the bathroom—primrose yellow in here, still sunshiny—she washed off her travel grime. Then she sat with her feet up on a chaise-longue that stood at the foot of the bed, and started to re-read her book on Paris.

When the phone rang she expected it would be an internal call, but she hoped it might be Peter. She gave her room number and name and the operator said,

'*Ne quittez pas, on vous appelle d'Angleterre.*'

From *England*? Nobody would be calling her from home unless something awful had happened, and when Betsy's voice came over the wire, 'Janna?' she gulped, and before she could ask, 'What is it?' Betsy said, 'I had to speak to you. Andy's just rung through from the office. I'm terribly sorry. It's very sad, isn't it?'

'What is?'

'Peter's father.'

'What about him?'

'Didn't you know he died on Tuesday?' Janna went stone·cold to the bone. 'Didn't you know?' Betsy repeated.

'He—didn't say anything about it.' The words jerked out, and she didn't recognise the voice as her own.

'He didn't?' Betsy couldn't understand that. 'I suppose he didn't want to worry you,' she said at last. 'I thought your holiday would be spoiled and you might be coming back early. I thought I'd better phone. Perhaps you are staying on, then?' She sounded as clear as though she was right here in the room. She would be wrinkling her nose now, puzzled.

'I'll let you know,' said Janna, as she replaced the receiver.

She went back to the chaise-longue and sat down again, gripping the velvet armrest with both hands, fingers digging in. It was very sad that Peter's father had just died, but the shock to Janna was that Peter had said nothing, and had shown no sign of distress or strain.

He had read those papers with total concentration, and he had gone now to listen to complicated business policies being discussed, his mind on nothing else because vast sums of money could depend on his expert advice.

He had never talked about his father, but even if they hadn't got on too well there should surely have been some regret, some emotion. But if there was it was put aside in one of those compartments in his mind.

It was inhuman to be so controlled. Her own father's death had prostrated her. She would miss him for the rest of her life, and Peter's lack of feeling horrified her.

This morning, when she had been jittery, she had thought—it will be all right when I reach Peter; and tonight he would be here with her, making her happy, making her love him. She would have given with no holding back, because his touch reached every nerve in her body, every cell in her brain. But she wouldn't have reached him because nobody could, and one day he would shut her out for ever.

Perhaps he would tell her tonight that his father had died. If he had told her this morning her sympathy and distress for him would have taken up time on the flight that he needed for studying those papers. Tonight he might spare a little time for sadness, but suddenly Janna couldn't face the prospect of tonight.

She couldn't stay here. After this holiday she would be committed. Peter wouldn't, but she would, and she didn't like the kind of man he was. That icy detachment of his appalled her. He admitted it. It was his strength, the cornerstone of his success, but she had never really seen it operating before. The day would come when it would operate against her, and if by that time she loved him it could be the finish of her.

She went to the phone and asked reception if there was any chance of them getting her on a flight to England as soon as possible. She'd take London, Birmingham or Manchester. She had had a phone call and she had to go home, she murmured something about a bereavement, and the woman who had answered said they would do their best.

She didn't want to be here when Peter came back to the hotel. She knew that was cowardly, but she also knew that no matter how hurt and angry her running away might make him tonight he would be ice-cool and competent tomorrow.

She was ashamed of herself, but she was saving herself, and she packed fast, folding clothes back into her case as though every second counted.

None of her clothes was new. She hadn't had time nor money to get anything new, but her nightdress was the prettiest she had, a pale pink cotton, and she crammed that into the case, never wanting to see it again.

A jilted bride must feel this way about her trousseau. Janna would never see that nightdress again without remembering how much she had wanted Peter to make love to her. She would have left it here, stuffed into the wastepaper basket, except that he might see it and what Freudian undertones would he make of that? As soon as she got home she would give it away, sell it, destroy it. Get rid of it somehow.

When she had packed she wrote a note for him, 'Sorry about your father, sorry about everything, I have to go home,' and left it on the dressing table. This was like something from a TV play, this was ridiculous. She was on the edge of hysterical laughter, or equally hysterical tears, it was so crazy, but she had to go.

Then she waited. And she was lucky, because they rang through quite soon to tell her a reservation had been secured on an afternoon flight from Charles de Gaulle airport to Heathrow.

She paid for the airline ticket and nothing was said about her account here. That was in Peter's name, and she would be settling that with him later, and whether the hotel staff believed her story about a bereavement or not they all looked and acted as though they did.

She was disgusted with herself, getting into this panicky mess. Allan had called her trip to Paris with Peter 'Midsummer madness.' It had been a Midsummer Night's Dream all right, and the waking was beastly. How she was going to explain to Allan and Betsy when she got back to the village she didn't know. She didn't know how she was going to explain to anybody.

She'd be a laughing stock. 'Back already?' they'd say. 'Back the day you went, not even stopping for one night in Paris. Did Mr Craig have to come back, then?'

When she came out of the station where Andrew had left her this morning it was drizzling with rain. It would be. That was the way this day had to end, with a wait of over two hours for the next and last bus out to the village, and no reply when she phoned the taxi rank.

It was a five-mile walk to Lower Egginton, along lanes with no footpaths, and so she dialled Betsy's number. Betsy would think she was out of her mind, but Betsy would collect her, and by now Janna was completely worn out.

She hadn't eaten since mid-morning. She hadn't thought about it and she certainly wasn't hungry, but her legs were like jelly and her head was throbbing.

Betsy answered; Janna was glad it wasn't Andy, she wasn't up to any explanations yet, all she wanted to say was, 'Please will you pick me up?' and she'd talk in the car.

'It's Janna——' she began, and Betsy shrilled,

'Where are you?'

'At the station. Our station.'

'What's going *on*? Peter's rung through. He said you were on your way home and would somebody ring him as soon as you got here? I told him I'd spoken to you earlier. Whatever have you come home for?'

'Will you pick me up?' asked Janna wearily.

'Yes.'

'Thanks.' She put down the phone. No one else was waiting to use it. She watched the mist of rain on the glass panels of the phone booth, and after a few minutes she went outside and stood in the rain because her forehead was hot and aching and the rain was cool.

Betsy's little car practically skidded to a halt. She had

come at a fair rate down the drive to the station, and she jumped out beside Janna, opening the boot and putting in the case, asking, 'What is this?'

'I had to come back,' said Janna.

'Why?'

Janna got into the passenger seat and Betsy, who wanted the mystery solved before she had to concentrate on driving through town, waited.

'It sounds crazy,' said Janna, 'but it was because he'd never even mentioned about his father.'

'You didn't know his father,' Betsy pointed out. 'He didn't have to tell you. It wouldn't have been much of a start for the holiday.'

'I don't think,' said Janna bitterly, 'he was being that considerate. How did he get on with his father, do you know?'

Betsy had told her that Peter's father was well-to-do, a landowner up North. Nobody had told her anything else about him and Betsy said, 'They must have got on all right, Peter used to go back home. Why?'

'Because,' said Janna, looking straight ahead, into the rain and the darkness and the parking lot by the station, lit by one dim lamp, 'he spent the flight going through business papers. He'd shut it out: his father, grief, everything. He didn't think about it. That's how he operates. Like Caroline said—there is no way anyone is ever going to break his heart.'

'Do you want to break his heart?' That was a silly question, but Betsy seemed to think that it was a silly situation, and Janna said,

'Of course I don't, and I wanted those three days in Paris, I wanted Peter.' She still wanted him terribly, perhaps she always would. 'But I don't like him,' she said doggedly, because that was why she had come back. 'He scares me. He doesn't really care for anyone. He's the hardest man I've ever met.'

Betsy switched on the ignition and started the engine,

driving into the almost deserted parking lot to turn the car. 'But you always knew that,' she pointed out. 'I mean, he's great to have on your side, and you'd have had a great time while it lasted. You said there was no danger in it for you.'

Janna huddled into her seat. 'There could be, I shouldn't have gone, I couldn't stay,' and Betsy sighed.

'You might have stayed long enough to say goodbye,' she said crossly, and Janna could understand Betsy's annoyance. She had made things awkward all round, running away from Peter in this melodramatic fashion.

'Sorry,' she said miserably, and Betsy sighed again, then softened.

'You must have had a rotten day.' she said. 'Will you come back to my place?'

'I want to go to the cottage, please. I don't think I could face Andy tonight,' and Betsy grinned ruefully.

'I shouldn't bother trying to explain to Andy, it's never going to make any sense to him.'

Judy was in the cottage. Betsy had called her in, and put down her food and milk, before Janna's call from the station. When the girls opened the front door the cat came to meet Janna.

'Somebody's glad I'm back,' she said, stroking Judy, and feeling her head swim as she bent down, so that she put a hand in front of her eyes and Betsy said,

'I'll make some tea.'

Janna sat on the floor stroking the cat, feeling so tired that everything would have to wait till tomorrow. All she could do tonight was drink that tea and undress and fall into bed. Tomorrow, when she was rested, she would face the future.

Betsy turned from switching on the kettle, and said, 'You've got to phone him. I said as soon as we heard from you I'd ring back, and now you're here you've got to speak to him.'

'Oh no,' Janna groaned. She closed her eyes and held

the cat tighter, and heard Betsy dialling, then waiting, then giving Peter's name.

'It's Betsy,' said Betsy. 'I'm speaking from the cottage. Janna's here.' She held out the receiver and Janna took it from her and said the only thing she could say.

'I'm sorry about this.'

'What's it all about?'

She had always liked the sound of Peter's voice on the phone. It had warmed her and cheered her, and made her feel that he was very close. But tonight it was cool and distant, and her stomach leaped and dropped as though she was facing an enemy. Peter would understand even less than Andy. Peter could be angry, and dangerous.

She said, 'I'm sorry about your father.'

'They told me about your bereavement,' he said drily. 'I'm at a loss to understand why my father's death should put you on the first plane back to England.'

'I——' Janna looked for Betsy, who had gone into the kitchen and couldn't have helped her anyway. She licked her dry lips, and tried to swallow, but her throat was too dry. She said, 'I shouldn't have gone to Paris with you. I don't want to start an affair. Not even a brief one. I thought I did, but I didn't, and when I got there——'

'It's a pity you didn't change your mind a little closer home,' he said caustically. 'In any case there was no need for you to carry on like an abducted Victorian. If sleeping with me suddenly became impossible I'd have got you another room. Another hotel if you'd have preferred it.'

He was understandably annoyed, but he didn't sound angry or deeply hurt, and she mumbled again that she was sorry.

'You made us look a couple of bloody fools,' he said, 'but it was your decision. It doesn't matter.'

It might not matter to him, but it had left her shaking

like a leaf and feeling wretched, and she didn't know how long that feeling would last. She whispered, 'I really am very sorry about your father.'

'Why?' he said. 'You never met him.'

He hung up first. He didn't say goodbye, and Janna put down the phone and then said, 'Goodbye,' because something had ended. Suddenly goodbye seemed the most terrible word in the world, and tears filled her eyes.

'What did he say?' Betsy asked.

'He thinks I'm a bloody fool.'

'So do I,' said Betsy.

Janna blinked and the tears squeezed through her lashes. She kept her back to Betsy who was saying, 'Everybody's going to ask what brought you back home again so soon. If I were you I should just tell them about Peter's father. No one around here will know that Peter hasn't come back too.'

'I don't care,' said Janna. 'It's nothing to do with anybody.'

'That's what I shall tell them anyway,' said Betsy. 'I've made the tea. I'll go and fetch Punch.'

Janna dried her eyes the moment she was alone, although she knew that as soon as she was really alone for the night she wouldn't be able to stop crying.

In the morning her pillow was damp and she was drained of tears and feeling. It had been a grisly night. She didn't know which had been worse, lying awake thinking, or the kind of dreams she had had when she tossed into troubled slumber. But when the alarm clock sounded, and she struggled to sit up and the day had started, she was sure that yesterday's decision had been the right one.

Now she had to stick to it. She was through with Peter, and he was certainly through with her. It would have been great while it lasted, but yesterday she had had a foretaste of the end of the affair. Remember that, she told herself.

Of course she wished she had never agreed to go to Paris, rushing back home, making such an exhibition of herself. But it had ended before she had fallen in love, and that was the right decision.

Today was Friday, three days to paint the cottage before opening the shop on Monday. That should keep her busy, and it was a job that badly needed doing.

She waited until Andrew would have left for work before phoning Betsy, then she said, 'Sorry about yesterday. I was a nuisance, wasn't I?'

'Yes,' said Betsy, honestly. 'How are you this morning? No regrets?'

'Only that I went in the first place.'

'Thank goodness for that,' said Betsy, 'because I don't think you'll get the chance to change your mind again.'

Peter was not likely to ask her again to go to Paris, or to go anywhere. She had made him look a fool too, and she knew it was finished. She said, 'It wouldn't have lasted. Probably not even the six months. I never was in Caroline's class anyway, and that's his class, isn't it? All dressed up and elegant, every time I went out with him. It wasn't me. Not really.'

'If you say so,' shrugged Betsy. Janna could hear McNaught squawking in the background. 'Ah well,' said Betsy with a little sigh, and then briskly, 'So what are you going to do today?'

'Could we fetch some more paint? I thought I'd start on the cottage.'

'Sure,' said Betsy promptly. 'I'll help.'

It was in Betsy's interests that the business started up again, but her help was genuine kindness and Janna said, 'You're a good friend.'

'I know I am,' said Betsy. She laughed, 'I ought to have a medal. But so are you,' she said. 'O.K., I'll be right along.'

They nearly filled the boot of the car with tins of emulsion and gloss, and while they were in town Janna bought food from a supermarket. If she went into the village store she would be given the third degree before she got out again, and there wasn't much to eat in the house. She hadn't expected to be home until late Sunday night. Her fridge contained the bare essentials of bacon, eggs and butter, and she stacked enough into a cardboard box to keep her going for the next few days.

No sooner were they at work—Janna doing the ceiling between the heavy black beams, Betsy roller-emulsioning a wall—than Mrs Moore walked in. She carried a shopping basket and she asked, 'Anything I can get for you?'

'I'm stocked up, thanks,' said Janna.

'Sorry about your holiday. That was bad luck.'

'Yes,' said Janna.

'How old was he?'

'Who?'

'Peter's father,' said Betsy. 'About sixty, I think.'

Mrs Moore shook her head, stayed long enough to say that even a couple of strokes of fresh paint made a difference, and then went off to do her shopping. 'What did you tell her?' Janna asked. 'And when?'

'I looked in last night.' Betsy went on rollering as she talked. 'I said that Peter's father had died suddenly, and there's the estate to be settled, a lot of property and that. He had to go to Paris on Thursday, so you just flew out with him for the day.'

'That's true enough,' Janna said drily.

Once Mrs Moore had told them in the village store everybody knew—or thought they knew—why Janna was back home. Several neighbours looked in to say they were sorry about Mr Craig's loss and the ruined holiday, and to admire the living room. By the end of the afternoon the furniture was back in place, McNaught was back in the kitchen, and the cottage was almost like home again.

'Come and eat with us?' Betsy offered, but she wasn't

surprised when Janna said she'd get herself a meal here. She suspected that Janna was still not too keen on facing Andy. 'I'll see you in the morning,' said Betsy.

Janna was walking round the paddock, with Freddy and Punch, when Allan appeared round the side of the house. He waved, looking pleased, and she came to him through the gate. 'I heard you were back,' he said.

'You heard right.'

They went into the kitchen. Allan must have come straight over, he was still carrying his evening newspaper. Someone must have told him as he walked from his garage to his cottage, and he had come here instead of home. 'Will you be going away again?' he asked.

He didn't think this was as simple as it sounded. He hoped there had been a disagreement, better still a quarrel, and when Janna said, 'No,' he whammed the newspaper down on the kitchen table in a gesture of triumph that had Punch's hackles rising and all his strong white teeth showing.

Janna said, 'All right, Punch, nobody's attacking the table.'

'Can I come over this evening?' asked Allan, with a nervous glance at the dog.

'Make it in about half an hour,' said Janna.

'You're a bad judge of character,' she scolded Punch as she went to get out of her paint-spattered overalls, and then she burst out laughing because he was looking at her for all the world as though he was saying, 'And you're not so hot yourself.'

She cooked sausages and tomatoes, and heated a small sponge pudding, which she and Allan ate together. It was like so many other evenings had been, except that she found it harder to talk to him.

She had to stop and think, hunting for subjects. He talked about school, pupils and colleagues, but his job had always bored him and she felt his boredom washing over her so that she had to stifle a yawn.

She covered it, putting up her hand to twiddle back a wisp of hair, and he said, 'A pity about your hair. I liked it longer. How long will it take to grow again?'

'A few months.'

In a few months the last few months should be a long way behind her. The shop should be stocked again. Allan would be walking into her home each night, or she would be going over to his. She wouldn't see Peter. His apartment would still be there, he would come and go, but she wouldn't see him, he would never come for her.

Agony twisted inside her, so savagely that she couldn't cry out. She sat, gripping her hands together under the table, while Allan finished his sponge pudding and told her he preferred her home cooking.

It wasn't going to be all that easy. She had been right to finish, but she was going to miss Peter. Although the pain would lessen as time went by, right now it hurt as though it would last for ever.


The customers came. On Monday it seemed that nearly every woman who had ever bought or sold at Janna's Place turned up with something to restock the shelves. Betsy and Janna greeted them all, so glad to see them and the clothes they brought with them that there was almost a party-time atmosphere.

The account of the fire must have been given fifty times. Everybody looked at Janna's hair and gasped, and laughed when Betsy told them how she had run out with the cat and the birdcage.

Betsy was doing the pricing with the customers—a figure was agreed on each item from which Janna would take ten per cent. Then Janna typed out the lists, two copies, which both she and the customer signed. The typing took time, because since it had been knocked across the room during the fire the typewriter had developed a habit of jumping ahead. As soon as the rush was over it would have to go in for repair. In the meantime Janna typed slowly, backspacing when the need arose.

She jammed the keys when Sylvia Laurence walked in, because she had never expected to see Sylvia here. Then she jumped up. 'Hello, how lovely! Whatever brought you?'

'Peter told me,' said Sylvia. 'And what a narrow escape you had.'

'When did he tell you?'

'Just after it happened.'

Of course. He wouldn't be talking about her now, asking Sylvia to help her. Because Sylvia had brought two large cases. 'I went round my friends,' she explained.

She was wearing a little plain black suit, but so beautifully cut, and her shoes and handbag were so obviously exclusive, that most of the women there decided they were interested in what those cases contained.

Janna was very grateful. She would have preferred not to get any deeper into Peter's debt, but it was Sylvia who had gone through her own wardrobe, and bothered her friends, and it was Sylvia she thanked, profusely and sincerely.

While they priced the goods in the living room Sylvia said, 'Sad about Peter's father, wasn't it?'

'Very,' said Janna.

'Do you know if he'll be keeping on the house? It's a beautiful old place.'

'I don't know.' She didn't know much about Peter's private life. She never had. She said, 'I—well, I don't think we'll be seeing each other again.'

'Oh, I am sorry.' Sylvia seemed surprised, and she sounded sorry, which was odd considering she had warned Janna against Peter.

When Allan came round that evening Janna took

him into the shop. She was thrilled with it. The security these goods represented made her feel that she was off to a flying start again.

'It looks as good as ever,' said Allan.

'It will be. Maybe even better.'

'That's what I was thinking.' Allan put an arm around her, and it was nice to lean against him and know what a good friend she had in him. 'I never told you,' he said, 'but your father invited me over here.'

'What?' Her father had never been much for visitors. Although there was no reason, of course, why he shouldn't have asked Allan to call.

With his arm still around her shoulders Allan led her away from the shop to the little settee in the living room, and sat her down sitting close beside her. 'I think he wanted us to meet,' he said.

Her father had never been a matchmaker, and she had always found her own admirers without any trouble, but she supposed it was possible. 'I think he'd have liked it if we'd fallen in love,' said Allan softly.

'Do you?' Janna guessed where this was going, but when he whispered,

'Darling, will you marry me?' she managed to look suitably surprised, and keep down the voice that was saying inside her, 'Never in a million years.'

# CHAPTER EIGHT

ALLAN was waiting for Janna to speak, and Janna was at a loss for words. Now she was back here, and life was back on the old tracks, perhaps there was nothing to stop them marrying. But it was too soon. She couldn't help it, she was still missing Peter. Allan should have had the sense to wait.

Although if he had it wouldn't have made any difference, because no matter how long he waited there was everything to stop them marrying. It wasn't on and it never would be. She could never be Allan's wife—she just knew that.

'You need looking after,' he told her, kissing her, and it was all she could do not to push him away. 'You need a man about the house.'

Not Allan. Except dropping in for a meal and a chat, and then going back to his own home. When Janna locked her door for the night she wasn't going to lock Allan inside with her. She was muttering something about this being very sweet of him, and how she appreciated being asked but she didn't want to get married, thank you.

'Think about it,' he urged. 'We've always got on so well, except for the last few weeks.' He was being magnanimous there, prepared to overlook her flirtation with Peter Craig. In fact it had made her more attractive to him. She had been unattainable for a while, and a glitteringly successful man had fancied her. 'I love you,' he said, and Peter had never said that, not even when he was asking her to go away with him.

She shook her head and pulled back, and Allan said, 'Just think about it anyway.'

She didn't need to give the matter any more consideration, but next morning she told Betsy that Allan had said how about them getting married as she needed somebody to look after her.

'Not by him,' said Betsy, who had brought her sewing equipment over and was plugging in her machine on the living room table. 'And you've got enough hangers-on with the bird and the donkey. Not to mention Punch and Judy.'

Certainly Allan took more than he gave, and Janna had been making his life easier ever since he came to live in Betsy and Andy's old cottage. She said, 'He said my father invited him over here to meet me. He thinks my father had him down as a son-in-law.'

'Nuts,' said Betsy. Several of the garments brought in yesterday needed very slight repairs, and she picked up a jacket with a buttonhole that had begun to unravel.

'Don't you believe him?' asked Janna.

'I'd say that was a load of rubbish,' said Betsy. 'It's like his book.'

That was what Janna thought, and she didn't notice that she wasn't defending Allan's masterpiece but taking up another point. 'Talking of spongers, I owe Peter some money. He paid for my air ticket and my hotel booking and I want him to have it back.'

Betsy pulled a thoughtful face and advised, 'I'd forget it if I were you, he doesn't need it.'

'I'd prefer to square accounts,' said Janna, and Betsy looked up suddenly, from selecting a needle from her sewing box.

'You'd do better to leave things as they are. Unless of course you feel you've simply got to see him again.'

'No!' Janna snapped. 'I do not feel I've got to see him. I just want to pay him.'

It wasn't quite time to open the shop, and she went to the kitchen tap to fill a small jug which she took into the shop to top up the two vases of yellow roses. Coming back with the empty jug she said casually, 'Any idea when he'll be over here?'

'No,' said Betsy.

'Would you leave a note in the apartment?'

'Yes,' said Betsy.

Janna sat down and wrote it right away. 'I'm sorry for the trouble I caused and although I don't see why you should make things any easier for me I'd be grateful if you'd let me pay for my ticket and my hotel bill. Please. Thank you for asking Sylvia to help us restock, she brought some beautiful things. I meant what I said on the phone, but it was very nice knowing you. Good luck always, J.'

Betsy's eyebrows rose. 'I just leave this in the apartment, do I?'

'Please.'

'What are you expecting?'

'I hope,' said Janna, 'he'll let me pay him. That's all.'

It was always possible they might bump into each other when Peter came to the village. It would be better to have a friendly finish to the affair and remain good neighbours. That was all she hoped or wanted. 'I think you've got a cheek,' said Betsy, but when Janna asked,

'Don't you want to leave it?' she grinned.

'I'll put it just inside the door and say you must have shoved it under.'

They did a week of brisk business. If anything the fire brought in more customers, and could have been a good publicity stunt. It was a good week in all.

On Wednesday evening Janna was in Betsy's kitchen, when Andrew came home from work. 'Hello,' she said brightly.

'How was Paris?' aked Andrew, and Janna blushed.

'I didn't see much of it.'

'Hardly worth taking the trip, was it?' said Andrew. 'I'll never understand women.' And that was all that was said about that.

But several times during the evening Janna caught herself nearly asking about Peter. The questions almost slipped out: had Andy seen him? he was back from France now, of course, what was he doing? It wasn't that she was concerned with Peter's affairs, but he must have become a sort of habit with her this last month or so because she had to keep checking herself from bringing him into the conversation.

She had to watch with Betsy too. She didn't want Betsy to think she was thinking about Peter, so she never mentioned him all week. Betsy would probably tell her if he was coming to his apartment, although often he gave no notice, just turned up and walked in, it was his home. She couldn't ask Betsy to warn her if he might be around, because then Betsy would say, 'You *do* want to see him,' and she didn't. She just felt that she would like to know.

Allan turned up and walked in most nights. He said, 'I'm not going to rush you for an answer,' and Janna said,

'But you've had an answer. Thank you, but no.'

'That's no answer,' said Allan.

He brought some typing over, including the pages that had been trampled during the fire, and she said, 'I will type them for you, but the machine's a bit dodgy. I'm taking it in next week.'

'I'll leave them with you, then,' Allan said, and there they stayed on the little side table in the living room.

On Friday a reporter and photographer arrived from one of the local newspapers that had carried Janna's S.O.S. advert, and she told them how everybody had rallied round to help after the fire. They took photographs of Janna and Betsy, inside and outside the shop, and one of Janna holding one of her father's paintings.

She had said, 'A friend suggested I might sell some of my father's pictures because I really needed the money.'

'Your father was an artist?' the reporter, a girl,

prompted, and Janna told them her father had been an art teacher, and it was wonderful that the pictures had been worth enough to save the day, because she hadn't known that, and she had never thought of trying to sell any of them before.

'Who was the friend?' the reporter asked, and after a moment Janna said,

'Peter.' But Peter Craig wouldn't want it implied that he might be backing Janna's Place, so she went on quickly, 'A neighbour. That's one of my father's paintings,' and she pointed to the wheatfields on the wall.

'We could have a shot of you holding that,' said the photographer.

When she closed her notebook the reporter went searching through the rails of clothes, buying a couple of dresses and promising to return with a suit she had slimmed out of.

'The story should be in a week today,' she said, and Betsy and Janna beamed at each other as they waved the press car goodbye, because a picture-spread would be worth more than half a dozen paid advertisements.

Then Betsy said, 'Peter's probably coming tomorrow night.'

'Oh?' Janna watched the car turn out of the lane.

'I don't know for sure,' added Betsy, 'but Andy said this morning that Peter had this business appointment round here tomorrow afternoon, so he could be staying in the apartment. If he is he'll get your note. You still want me to leave it around?'

'I still want to get out of his debt, yes,' said Janna.

It was the first time she had mentioned Peter all week, and she wondered if Betsy had thought her voice sounded strained when she did because Betsy was looking very hard at her.

On Saturday evening Janna had the week's accounts to bring up to date, so she told Allan that she was going to be busy and that she couldn't go to the cinema. Allan would have taken her out more these days, but she was busier than she had ever been. Of course she had to keep the books straight, and the women whose clothes had sold this week would be expecting their cheques.

'Can I come over?' Allan asked, but she said she would rather he didn't.

'I'll get on faster on my own. Anyone else around would be a distraction.'

So she was alone when she was doing her accounts, and it had been a very healthy week for profits. But she was tense, it had been hectic, and several times she had to get up and pace around the room because she couldn't settle comfortably.

She put on a cassette for some soothing background music, and caught herself listening instead of totting up the rows of figures. But the accounts were done at last, and the cheques written out, and then she decided to type a few pages for Allan, to make up for not going to the cinema with him. If she typed slowly perhaps the typewriter wouldn't jump.

She typed very slowly, and she must have lost the thread of the story over the past weeks because tonight the characters seemed unreal. She thought—it isn't very good. Bits of it are all right, but it's no masterpiece. Oh dear, poor Allan. But she went on typing until it was time for bed.

She called Judy in from the back door, and let Punch out, then went down the little path of garden to where she could see the lights in the top floor of the Old Vicarage that meant Peter was home. It wouldn't be Betsy as late as this.

He would have read her note and she supposed that might have been why she'd wanted to be alone here tonight, because if Peter had come across it might have been embarrassing to have an audience. Perhaps he had only just arrived. If he had he might still phone her.

But he might not be alone. Caroline could be with him.

Or another Caroline. And good luck to them, because Janna had just walked out of that kind of a relationship, but she hoped he would phone her, or come across, or answer her note somehow because the desire to pay off every penny she owed him was becoming something of an obsession.

She dreamt that the phone was ringing. It was so vivid that she was out of bed and half across the room before she realised that it was a dream. That this was some unearthly hour in the deepest depth of the night and there wasn't any sound at all.

Peter came next morning, knocking on the front door as she was peeling the potatoes in the kitchen, and she answered with the peeler in her hand and her hands wet. He wore a camel cashmere polo-necked sweater and beautifully cut brown slacks. His smile was that slow boyish grin that would disarm anyone who didn't know him for a complicated and dangerous man. 'I got your note,' he said. 'Are you in a position already to be paying debts that haven't been called in?'

Her note had amused him. It probably was rather comic from a girl who was almost broke, but Janna didn't smile. 'No,' she said. 'Not really.'

'Then take my advice and wait until you're asked for the money. May I see round?'

'Why not?' She stepped back. Her hands felt clammy and she realised she hadn't even stopped to dry them when she'd heard the knock on the door.

The living room looked shining clean and bright. 'You've worked hard,' he commented. 'It looks splendid.'

'I had a lot of help. Betsy mostly.'

It wasn't splendid, it was only white paint, but she wanted to take his arm and show him every room and say, 'Isn't it super? Isn't it as good as new? Please will you stay to dinner?'

It was a pity she couldn't have Peter just as a friend, because there was no one who made her feel more alive. His approval of the way she had cleaned up the mess had her blushing with pleasure as though he was paying her wild and extravagant compliments.

She opened the door to show him the shop. 'Such a lot of stock came in,' she said. 'People were wonderful. Sylvia brought some lovely things.' She rubbed her damp hands on her denim skirt and touched a mint-green dress on a hanger, and thought that if she had still been going around with Peter she might have bought this for herself and worn it today. It would have brought out the green glints in her eyes.

She wished he would say, 'What are you doing this afternoon?' but that was dangerous thinking, and he was dangerous, standing so near. She couldn't be near him without feeling that physical pull as though she had moved into a magnetic field, and he knew it. He must know because he was looking at her, very still, as though he was hardly breathing, letting the tension mount between them until she nearly cried out.

When she couldn't have borne the silence a second longer he turned and went back into the living room, stopping by the desk, to look down at the manuscript. 'Still doing the typing?' he asked.

'Yes.' He was reading it and she said, 'I'd rather you didn't start criticising that. Allan's a good friend of mine.' He had his back to her and this wasn't going to bother him, and she didn't even know why she was saying it, but she said, 'We may be getting married.'

He finished reading the page and put it on the top of the pile. Then he said, 'No, I don't think so,' and Janna thought at first he was talking about something he had read.

But he was speaking about her and Allan, with a calm authority that was the height of insolence. As though he was in charge, and she needed his permission. It was nothing to do with him, she hadn't asked his advice, and she would have pointed that out, but he said, 'Well, good morning,' and smiled at her and let himself out of the front door.

He had such conceit. Even though she had walked out on him in Paris he thought she was still here if he wanted her. He knew that had been a panic flight because she was scared, and that she still longed for him to love her, and he knew that she would never run to Allan. He didn't think she would marry Allan and neither did she, but he had no right to know her so well when she hardly knew him at all.

She went back to peeling the potatoes, hacking great hunks out of them. She was so rattled that she had no patience for fastidious peeling.

Betsy phoned about lunch time and asked, 'Can you talk? Are you on your own?'

'Allan's coming over any time,' said Janna.

'You haven't heard anything from Peter?'

'He called. But he won't let me pay him.'

Betsy was putting this casually, trying to pretend she wasn't all that curious. 'Did he say anything else? Are you——?'

'No, he didn't and no, we aren't,' said Janna. 'I offered him the money and he declined it so that debt's paid,' and she hung up before Betsy could think of any other way of angling her questions.

Betsy didn't ask any questions next day. She waited to see if Janna had anything to tell her, and when Janna talked about anything and anybody except Peter Betsy sighed and decided it really was over.

Anyhow Janna seemed happy enough, and both girls were busy. The booming business of last week had settled down, but there was still a steady stream of customers, and the write-up in Friday's paper could well bring them flocking again next week.

Sylvia Laurence came in on Thursday, with a few more clothes—most of the earlier ones she had brought had sold. She stayed for a cup of coffee and Janna went out to the car with her. As she settled herself behind the wheel Sylvia asked, as though the idea had just struck her, 'When did you last have a holiday?'

'Oh, a year ago.' Janna smiled. 'No, it must be two. Why?'

'The end of next month we're flying out to the cruiser, it's moored at Palma. Why don't you come too? For a day or two. Or a week or two.' She liked Janna. She liked the guts and the gaiety of the girl. 'My son and his wife will be there,' she said. 'So there'd be young company for you.'

'Thank you very much, that is kind of you.' Janna was surprised and flattered. It sounded like a dream holiday. If everything was in hand here by then and Betsy would look after the shop. 'May I think about it?' she asked.

'I'll be in some time next week,' said Sylvia, and Janna hesitated.

'I suppose—Peter won't be there, will he?'

'I shouldn't think so,' said Sylvia.

'Then I'd love to come. If I can fix things up here.'

She went back to tell Betsy and Betsy said it sounded a marvellous offer. 'She's nice,' said Betsy. 'I'll mind the shop.'

On Friday the local paper did them proud. They had almost a whole page to themselves, an account of how Janna's Place had 'risen like a phoenix from the ashes' with the help of good neighbours and friendly customers. The bit about the phoenix started Janna and Betsy laughing, it sounded very grand for a second-hand clothes shop. And the picture of them—with Freddy leaning over the fence—captioned 'Janna and Betsy with a friend' seemed even funnier. But it was all first class publicity, and the reporter did say that the goods were high quality and excellent value and Janna's Place was a place for bargains.

Janna showed Allan the paper as soon as he came

round that night, and he said, 'I've seen it.' He didn't sound impressed, nor amused, but then it always had taken a lot to amuse Allan.

'Don't you think Freddy takes a good photograph?' she asked, trying to make him smile, and he frowned at the picture he was looking at—Janna holding her father's painting. There was a paragraph which said, 'A friend suggested I might sell some of my father's paintings, and that was a very bright idea because the money they brought in started the business off again.'

Allan knew it had been Peter's suggestion, but seeing him given the credit, even though his name wasn't mentioned, seemed to be riling Allan. He said huffily, 'You don't need to feel so grateful to Craig. He probably conned you over those pictures.'

'*What?*'

'How do you really know what they were worth? One man comes along, a friend of his, and you take the first offer you're made. You don't tell me you got a fair deal. A man like Craig would cheat his own grandmother.'

That was so absurd that she should have laughed. Allan was jealous of Peter, that was all that meant. She knew she had been well paid, she had no doubts there, and she should have felt sorry for Allan. But instead she was angry—blazingly angry, as though he had put a match to a keg of dynamite. She had never raised her voice to Allan before, but suddenly she was yelling at the top of her voice, 'How *dare* you? How dare you make that kind of accusation when you know you're talking rubbish? Of *course* Peter didn't cheat me, and what do you mean—cheat his own grandmother? You want to watch it, my lad, or you're going to find yourself being sued for slander!'

She stopped then to draw breath, and she was actually looking around for something to throw. But there was no need to say any more or do anything because Punch, under the impression that Janna had finally got the message about Allan, bit him.

Allan went mad. It might have been better if he had stood still instead of leaping around, but that was hard to say for sure. Perhaps if he had Punch would have got an even better grip before Janna shrieked 'Punch, *no*!' and the slight scratch on Allan's leg could have been deeper. As it was his trouser leg was practically ripped off, just below the knee, and he was up on the table with Punch crouched for a spring.

Janna flung herself on the dog, grabbing him, holding him down. He was growling and snarling, but not at her, and Allan was inspecting his leg and gibbering, 'That animal should be put down. He's crazy—probably rabid! I'll not set foot in this house again until you've got rid of him.'

Making sure that Janna still had a stranglehold on Punch, he got down from the table and shot out of the door, his torn trouser leg flapping.

Then she started to shake; it had been quite frightening. 'You fool of an animal!' She shook Punch, who had the nerve to wag his tail. 'Oh, you *idiot*!' She wondered what the law was about dogs attacking people. She'd ask Andy. She'd go across to Betsy's because she was beginning to feel worried and slightly sick.

'What on earth——?' exclaimed Betsy when she opened the door to Janna's knock. 'You're white as a sheet. What's happened now?'

'I've just had a nasty moment. Punch has just bitten Allan.'

'Oh dear!' After a quick check that Allan wasn't walking wounded behind Janna Betsy brought her in, and Janna babbled,

'It only looked a scratch, but he tore his trouser leg. Allan's scared of dogs. He doesn't get on with them, you know how he's always been with Punch. He couldn't make me get rid of Punch, could he?'

Andrew looked up from an armchair in front of the television and said, 'Old Punch isn't a dangerous dog, he wouldn't attack for nothing. What happened?'

'Me,' said Janna as she flopped on to the settee. 'I started shouting and Punch thought I was having a row with Allan. Well, I was. He said that Peter swindled me over my father's paintings, that they were worth more than the dealer gave me.'

Andrew's pleasant round face went bright red. 'He'd better not go around repeating that.'

'That's what I told him. Of course it wasn't true.' But Andrew was looking as uncomfortable as though he knew something that made it hard to meet Janna's eyes and she faltered, 'It couldn't be, could it?' because that was a dreadful thought. 'But Peter does make money, doesn't he?' she heard herself say. 'He is an opportunist isn't he?' and Andrew bounced to his feet and roared furiously,

'It bloody well could not be true! On the contrary.'

'On the contrary?' she echoed.

From the corner of her eye she saw Betsy making some sort of signal, but Andrew wasn't looking at Betsy, he was glaring at Janna. 'I mean that if you call in another expert you'll get a more realistic offer, if you get an offer at all,' he said.

There was silence. Betsy gestured again, a shrug and a dropping of limp hands that said—Now you've said so much get on with it.

'All right, I'll tell you,' said Andrew. 'If this is what Allan Haines is going around saying. Peter must have bought those paintings, and told the dealer what to offer you. Because after they brought in tidy sums I thought the one your father gave us ought to be insured, and I had it valued and I was told it was worth a fiver at the most.'

Janna stared. She felt her jaw dropping and locking,

and open-mouthed she turned to Betsy. Betsy gave a very small nod and said in a small voice, 'You didn't want to take a loan off Peter, did you?'

'But I *have*.' At the moment that seemed to matter more than the fact that her father's work wasn't commanding real money, and she wailed, 'What am I going to do?'

'Forget it.' Andrew was still bitter. He went on with heavy sarcasm, 'Look on it as legal aid—Peter does a lot of that, you know. He isn't always making money. But no, of course you wouldn't know. Well, now you can go back and tell Allan Haines.'

'Oh, do shut up, dear,' said Betsy. 'She's upset.' And she went to sit down beside Janna and put an arm around her.

'So she should be,' growled Andrew, and stamped off into his office, banging the door behind him.

Betsy apologised for him. 'Sorry about that, but he really does admire Peter.'

'I'm beginning to understand why,' said Janna. 'But how am I going to pay him back?' She wasn't off to a flying start again, she was bogged down in debt.

'Do you have to say you found out?'

'Yes, I do.'

'Well, you can't pay anybody yet,' said Betsy reasonably.

'When's he coming?

'Tomorrow.'

Janna sat up straight, struck by an idea that she herself found quite appealing. 'And I don't have the money to hand back, and I don't suppose he needs a two-fingered typist. But how about a cook? I started off cooking for him, didn't I?'

'Yes.' Betsy looked hesitant. 'You could get a meal for him for tomorrow night, I suppose, but when he comes he might not be on his own.'

She meant some other girl might be with him, and Janna said firmly, 'I'm just offering to do the cooking to start paying off what I owe. I wouldn't dream of starting an affair again, I couldn't stand that.'

'O.K. then,' said Betsy. 'Fine. Yes. Why not?'

Saturday was a worrying day. It had been a shock hearing about the paintings. It was sad that the dealers didn't think her father's work was worth much, but Janna did and always would. They were beautiful pictures, and one day she would buy them all back from Peter, and keep them here in her home where they belonged.

She was nervous about tonight, but she couldn't think of any other way of starting to square accounts. Peter was due back at the Old Vicarage some time during the evening, Betsy didn't know when, and Janna went up to his apartment after she'd closed the shop.

She took a savoury flan and a salad, because perhaps she'd had better ask before she started cooking again in Peter's kitchen, and she laid the table for one. If anyone else came with him, or if he suggested Janna might stay for supper, then it would be easy enough to set another place. But one setting at the table struck the right note, she felt, that she was working off money owed.

When the table was set, and the food was waiting in the kitchen, there was nothing for her to do. She could have left it with a note, but it would be easier to explain in person, so she hung around, not quite confident enough to switch on television or hi-fi. She didn't want to look as though she was making herself at home again. Things had changed since she was living here.

There was no reason why she shouldn't have switched on the lights, and she would have done, of course, before it got dark. But when dusk started to creep in she was sitting at the turret window, in the dining end of the room, and the shadows behind her seemed restful and soothing.

She saw Peter's car come up the drive and go round to

the back of the house, and her heart started beating
like a bongo drum. Perhaps she should have left a note,
but it was too late now, so perhaps she should get up
and switch on the lights and get ready to explain why
she was here.

But her legs didn't feel too steady, and she huddled
back in the little alcove of the turret window, hoping that
he would come in alone. Not that it really mattered, but
when she heard the key turn, and saw him down the
other end of the room, and he shut the door and there was
no one else, she heard herself whisper, 'Thank God!'

He didn't turn on the lights right away. He went across
to the big green velvet armchair, and sat down, head
back and eyes closed. He looked tired, as though all
emotion had been washed out of him, and Janna started
to walk towards him.

He opened his eyes then and she said, 'I have to
talk to you.'

Then he sat up, and gestured that she should sit down
on the settee opposite, and she said, 'You bought my
father's paintings, and they weren't worth much, were
they?'

He shrugged. 'Did you get the rest valued?'

'In a way. That was kind of you, but now I owe you
rather more than my ticket to Paris, and I've been
thinking of ways to pay you.'

Peter chuckled, a glint of mischief in his eyes. 'This
sounds intriguing,' and she sounded stiffer than she
wanted to sound.

'I could cook meals for you.'

'You could indeed.'

'So when you're coming, if you'll let me know. Or
Betsy.'

'I'll do that. Do I get a meal tonight?'

'I brought a flan.' She was getting up when he said.
'Not yet. Sit down. How is everything?'

She told him how everything was. Trade good,

prospects promising. She told him that Sylvia had called and invited her to go on holiday, and he said, 'Shall you?' almost as though he knew about it. Although it was probably wishful thinking to wonder if he might be going too, and to remember Sylvia's smile when she'd said, 'I shouldn't think so.'

She told him about the newspaper story, 'a phoenix rising from the ashes,' and he laughed at that. 'We had four pictures in all,' she said. 'Everybody thought it was terrific.'

Except Allan, and she said, 'Punch bit Allan on Friday night.'

'Why?' asked Peter drily. 'Did Punch read the book?'

'That could explain it,' she said, 'but it was because I was shouting. Allan said you'd cheated me on the paintings, they were worth more, and Punch thought it was anybody's fight.'

'But you knew I hadn't cheated you?'

'I must have done or I shouldn't have yelled at Allan. And then Andy told me their picture was valued at five pounds.'

'Andy,' said Peter, 'should mind his own business,' and she said warmly,

'I'm glad he told me. I like it in here. I'm glad I can come back again.'

'You never went away,' said Peter, and as she blinked in the half light, 'You're with me wherever I am, because I'm in love with you.'

That sounded wonderful, but he didn't mean what she meant by love, and she said quietly, 'You mean you want me. But you don't know me. Oh, you know more or less how I'll react. You know that—"

How could she explain? Her fingers wove together and tightened as she sat there, feeling so empty, so cold, so terribly lonely. 'You know that I fancy you,' was pathetically inadequate, but she said it because she could hardly say, 'You are the heartbeat of my life,' although in that moment she had stopped deluding herself. That was how she felt about him.

She even managed a little laugh. 'When we first met you didn't really notice me until I dressed up to go out with the Laurences. That's when I caught your attention and you decided I was presentable.'

'I'd decided you were more than that before then. When I'd seen you out in the paddock, from the window.' He smiled at her gasp. 'It might have been the donkey too, but I looked out for you most nights I was here. And Betsy talked about you. About the business and the animals. She didn't know I wanted to meet you, but if you hadn't walked out of her kitchen I'd have thought up some other way.'

Caroline was here then. Caroline was sleeping in the big bed, and Janna asked wryly, 'Because Caroline was starting to be a nuisance, and you were due for a change?'

'You think Caroline was a nuisance?' He looked steadily at her, an eyebrow lifted. 'I've never known a woman as big a nuisance as you.'

'Do I bother you?' So she had been a nuisance, but not in Caroline's way. She had never turned possessive, badgered him to marry her.

Oh, she had run in Paris, but as soon as she'd got away she'd left that note about the money. That was to get him to come to her house. Or phone her. She said, 'I dreamt you phoned in the dead of night. I jumped out of bed because I thought you were calling me,' and he said,

'I was. It was twenty minutes past three, if the time's of any interest to you.' All that interested her was why he had phoned and then hung up, but she waited and Peter went on, 'I couldn't sleep. I knew it was common sense to wait till morning, but I wanted to hear you speak. Only as soon as I dialled I lost my nerve.'

Janna couldn't believe that. '*You* lost your nerve?'

It was the time of no-colour, when everything seems varying shades of grey. When you can't hear too clearly, and the man in the green-grey chair was sitting so still that she had to strain to hear him. Which was nonsense, although she was straining to hear, holding herself tight, holding her breath.

He said, 'I thought at that time in the morning you'd probably hang up and that would have hurt like hell. If I went to your house I thought I'd stand a better chance of seeing you and talking to you. I'd have been round again this weekend, tomorrow.'

She supposed she should be flattered that her rejection could hurt him. He hated to lose. He'd hate to be rejected. But he could do more than hurt her. He could wreck her life, and he might do just that, because no one had ever said he was a gentle man.

'Why did you leave me in Paris?' he asked suddenly, and so harshly that she shrank instinctively, as though she was under interrogation, and stammered,

'When I heard about your father, and you'd said nothing, I thought that if you could shut out grief like that you could shut me out. Well, you can, can't you? You can close doors in your mind. You told me.'

'Not on you.' He leaned forward, gesture and voice impatient as though he was stating something she should have known. 'On everything else but you.' Then he sat back and his voice was controlled again, a lawyer summing up a situation. 'I was very young when I knew I wasn't wanted. There were servants about, I was looked after, but my mother was busy with her social life and her lovers, and my father was into politics in those days.

'I was at boarding school from the earliest age they'd take me, and neither of them ever came near. No visits, no letters. So I stopped thinking about them when I was at school. I always seemed able to do that, say, "I won't think about it," and concentrate on something else.

During the holidays they were mostly away. They did a lot of going away. Rarely together, and never with me.'

. . . 'Don't go away,' he had said to her, and that first day, 'Please don't run.' Perhaps he did need her, although she had thought that no one in the world could get really close to him. Janna was sure he had told no one else what he was telling her now . . .

'My mother was killed in a car crash when I was fourteen. I was sorry, but I could shut it out, tell myself, "I'll cry later." And in the end I didn't cry at all. It was the same when my father died, although we'd got along well enough for years.

'It's a useful knack, doors in the mind.' The self-mockery was in his voice now. 'It sharpens the concentration and you waste no energy. I'm well known for it.' Then the mockery went. 'But I can't shut doors on you. You open them all. I wish you'd stayed in Paris. We should have had to come back early, but we should have been together there,' and Janna asked fiercely,

'Would you have given me a golden bracelet like you bought Caroline the first time you made love to her?' as she realised how deep and primitive her jealousy ran. She couldn't share him. Once he was her lover they would belong to each other and she could never let him go without tearing herself apart.

He said quietly, 'It sounds trite—it would be different with you; but it always has been. You've been in my blood and my bones from the beginning. You're the one who'll always matter more than my life. It's that simple.

'I didn't want to give you a bracelet, I wanted to give you a ring. I thought that if I asked you to marry me in Paris you might say, "Yes." Paris is supposed to have a kind of magic, isn't it?'

He wasn't sure of her. In the shadows she saw the uncertainty and the pleading in his face, and he had to be sure because she could break his heart. She knew that, and she held out her arms, then she was in his arms as she was in his heart, fitting so wonderfully, so close, so right.

Peter tilted her face to look into her eyes. 'You will marry me?'

'Oh yes,' she said, and smiled. 'Well, you knew I couldn't marry Allan.'

'No, you couldn't,' he agreed, 'I'd have killed him first,' and she laughed, although that could possibly have been true.

'What am I getting myself into? You're a peasant, you're a barbarian.'

He smiled, 'The civilised skin doesn't go too deep,' then his smile stilled and he looked at her with wonder and love. 'I want to give you everything,' he told her. 'What can I give you? Do you want a manor house? You said you didn't, but perhaps you should see my old home before we decide whether to keep it.'

She didn't know whether they would keep it, she didn't care. There was only one thing in the world she wanted. 'I want you to love me,' she said, and he kissed her, slowly and deeply, and began to caress her; and the touch of him, the hardness of his skin against hers, brought a surge of joy deep inside her and a release like a flower blossoming and opening, and she held him and loved him as they would always hold and love each other. For they belonged together. He was her lover, strong and passionate, fierce and tender, the one for all seasons and all needs. And those who said he was not a gentle man did not know him at all.

# The Warrender Saga

## The most frequently requested series of Harlequin Romances . . . Mary Burchell's Warrender Saga

| | |
|---|---|
| A Song Begins | The Curtain Rises |
| The Broken Wing | Song Cycle |
| Child of Music | Music of the Heart |
| Unbidden Melody | |
| Remembered Serenade | |
| When Love Is Blind | |

Each complete novel is set in the exciting world of music and opera, spanning the years from the meeting of Oscar and Anthea in *A Song Begins* to his knighthood in *Remembered Serenade*. These nine captivating love stories introduce you to a cast of characters as vivid, interesting and delightful as the glittering, exotic locations. From the tranquil English countryside to the capitals of Europe—London, Paris, Amsterdam—the Warrender Saga will sweep you along in an unforgettable journey of drama, excitement and romance.

# The Warrender Saga

## The most frequently requested Harlequin Romance series

# Complete and mail this coupon today!